Prairie Pictures

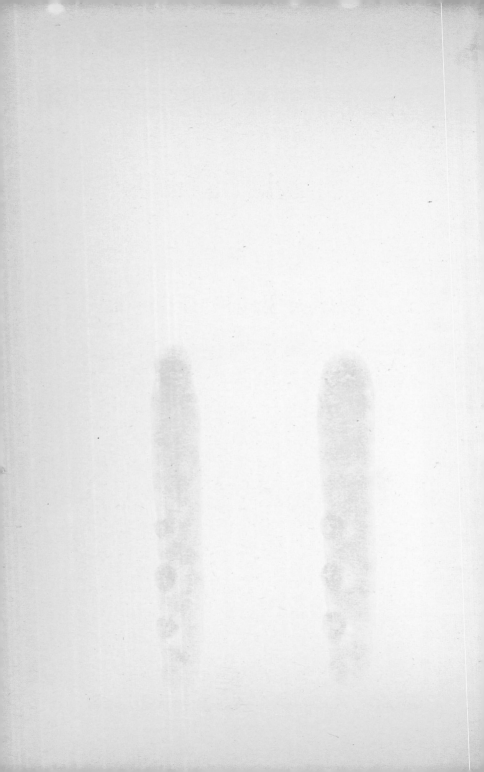

Prairie Pictures

by

Shirlee Smith Matheson

M&S

Canadian Cataloguing in Publication Data

Matheson, Shirlee Smith
Prairie pictures

ISBN 0-7710-5857-8

I. Title.

PS8576.A88P73 1989   jC813'.54   C88-095067-6
PZ7.M38Pr 1989

Printed and bound in Canada

McClelland & Stewart Inc.
The Canadian Publishers
481 University Avenue
Toronto, Ontario
M5G 2E9

To Hayley and Britt

Contents

1
New Promises

The town hung like a necklace of costume jewellery from the shoulders of the Trans-Canada highway. Service stations, tire stores, convenience marts. We looked at them in turn, craning to peer the farthest so we would be the first to spot something interesting.

I was twelve the day we moved to Gardin, my younger sister Bonnie just six. It was our third move that year.

"Where the devil is 'Greenborough'?" Dad pulled the station wagon sharply into the parking lot of an Esso station. "You can't find anything in a two-bit town like this! Nothing's marked." He stomped into the garage and we could see him questioning a beak-capped attendant. He came slamming out, gunned the car into Drive and we spun away shooting gravel.

Our new home was located in the Greenborough Subdivision, 122 Greenborough Drive. Dad turned off the main road, past a chicken farm whose stench told us that although we would be living in town we were really quite rural. He then made an abrupt right and suddenly all the street signs began with the word "Green."

Greenborough Drive was a canal of brown mud. Bales of straw had been scattered under parked cars to keep them from sinking. Slippery concrete sidewalks led to grey stucco houses; none of the houses had porches or shutters or anything to make them look nice. I glanced sideways at Bonnie and she looked back at me. Tears glinted in the corners of her big blue eyes. I slid over and patted her on the shoulder.

We had been lucky to find a place to rent, Dad had told us, as the town was growing so quickly there was very little available. The managers of the new packing plant had spotted an ad in the paper for a building permit, phoned the owners, and reserved six duplex units for their foremen.

We pulled over to the curb fronting 122 Greenborough Drive and felt the station wagon swerve as the wheels caught in a rut of mud. "Jesus Murphy!" Dad said through clenched teeth. Mom said nothing. She held the dog, petting him right over his eyes, as if she were thinking of other times, of other places.

Bonnie and I slid to the right side of the car and stepped out carefully. Already the back wheel had sunk nearly to the hubcap in the brown clay. We took big steps, trying to stay balanced as we tripped up the walk to our new house.

Dad opened the door and almost toppled backward as the flimsy aluminum screen door was suddenly caught by the wind. It whipped in gusts between the duplexes and howled around the corner, as if angry to find houses blocking its sweep over the flat prairie.

Bonnie and I removed our running shoes and stepped inside. The house wasn't quite finished. Smells of silicone and paint filled the air. Plumbing tools had been left in the bathroom, and the top of the toilet tank was still wrapped in paper. Brown water spurted from the taps when I turned them on.

"I wanna go home!" Bonnie whimpered.

Mom bent to comfort her. "Sssshh, sssshh, this *is* home, sweetie. We'll get settled real soon. You and Sherri will like it here. You'll see how nice this place is." Her voice sounded strange as it echoed through the empty rooms.

"I booked us a motel room for the night," Dad said. "The furniture will be here in the morning. Let's go."

As we drove over to the motel Dad told us, "The other packing plants are on strike, so ours will be working round-the-clock shifts."

Mom sighed.

"It won't be forever," Dad said quickly, then added irritably, "Anyway, I'm the one who's doing the work."

We proceeded in silence to the motel, only stopping to order a bucket of chicken to take with us.

The sun was barely breaking over the horizon when I saw Dad's shadow moving around on the far side of the room, heard him splashing in the bathroom, then, click, he was gone. He didn't return until after we were in bed in our new house.

We had a month before school started so Bonnie and I helped Mom set up the house, then spent our afternoons playing games: *Clue*, *Snakes and Ladders*, *Chinese Checkers*. We started a big 400-piece jigsaw puzzle of a sailing ship, but Bonnie lost interest because there were too many blue sky and water pieces. We would sometimes hear kids yelling a couple of streets away and once, on a walk around the block, two girls our age walked past us, but we didn't get to know anyone.

It was difficult to play outside. Our yard was a patch of the same brown clay that rutted the front streets. The landlord promised us topsoil and instant lawn, but weeks went by and the only green came from tufts of couch grass and dandelions. On days when the weather was dry the clay would sift like fine brown icing sugar dusted up by the prairie wind, entering beneath the doors and windows, coating everything. We could feel it in our noses and in our eyes. When it rained it turned into sticky mud that sucked our boots right off our feet. Cars would go slowly down the street, their wheels growing larger and larger, until finally the driver would have to stop and poke the gumbo with a shovel until the wheels could turn again.

Our dog was not let out unless absolutely necessary. Then we had to tie him to the gas meter at the back of the house where he whined and yelped and stood shaking with misery in the wet clay. When we finally brought him in, his brown fur would be coated with hardened chunks and the bathtub water would swirl like a muddy river.

One hot afternoon in late August Bonnie and I were sitting outside on the concrete steps playing with our Barbie dolls when a pickup truck pulled up to the duplex next to ours. Two guys jumped out and began hauling in a mattress. Their door faced ours across a six-foot expanse of clay, and although the men looked at us as they passed, they said nothing. Bonnie became nervous, ducking her head down so all I could see was a whirl of blond hair.

The men had bushy unshaven faces and dirty hands. I watched to see what they owned: cardboard boxes overflowing with clothes, a jumble of rubber boots caked with mud, two stained mattresses, a table and three chairs, a heavy old-fashioned couch, its dark-red upholstery stained almost black. They went away for another load. In came the hugest stereo speakers I had ever seen, taller than me. Then the rest of the stereo, modern silver and black pieces that must have cost a lot of money. They passed us without a word, hauling in box after box of records, allowing their aluminum screen door to slam in our faces each time they brought in another load.

Finally, when they were finished, one of the men came outside and stood on the edge of his step, looking west toward the front road. I followed his gaze, but could see nothing except their mud-spattered pickup truck. He scratched his chest, reaching inside his red flannel shirt to give himself a really good going-over. He glanced over at us, sniffed, then went back inside.

Bonnie crept into the house and I followed, stuffing the Barbies into their box.

"Come on, Bonnie, let's play dress-up," I said, but she murmured softly, "I don't want to, Sherri," and sat down in front of her bookshelf, pulling out a fairy tale. I pretended to start the game, pinning my long brown hair in a bun like an old lady's, getting out our set of play make-up.

I was small for my age, and people often thought I was no more than ten. My eyes were large and blue like Bonnie's but people said I had a serious look. Bonnie was always smiling.

"Come on, I'll paint your nails green," I said, arranging our make-up in a row on her little table.

"Okay." She came over and sat on a chair, holding out her grubby hands. Her nails were short and chewed.

"Hold still." I pretended to examine them critically, as I had seen a manicurist do to Mom's hands. That was when we lived in the city and Mom used to have her hair styled and nails manicured every week.

As I painted Bonnie's fingernails, I thought of when we lived in Calgary, our second-last place, in a big bungalow-style house with a huge yard. A poplar tree that must have been fifty years old towered over one corner of the back yard. The first spring Dad threatened to cut it down when sticky buds dropped onto the hood of his car, marring the paint, but Bonnie and I cried so he relented. He later fixed a swing for us from a big branch of the tree, and Bonnie and I spent hours swinging back and forth under the bright dancing leaves. We lived there three years. Then we had moved to Saskatchewan.

I finished Bonnie's fingernails, then watched as Bonnie took the dog's front paws, one at a time, and carefully painted his mud-caked toenails the same lime-green as her own. "There," she said. "Now he looks like he's standing on a lawn instead of dirty old mud." The dog looked at his feet, making a half-attempt to lick at the bright spots, then seemed to think better of it. I ruffled his ears, then stood up and walked over to look out the bedroom window. The landscape was the same colour as the sky, grey-brown. It was going to rain. I turned back to Bonnie.

"It'll be okay," I said, as if reading her thoughts. "We'll get to know kids at school. You'll like school. It's like kindergarten, only more fun."

Bonnie nodded, examining the green shiny dots of colour at the ends of her fingers. I looked out again. Sure. It could be no better or worse than the three other places where we lived in the last year. Three schools: Calgary, Regina, now Gardin, back in Alberta. I wondered if I would find a friend here. I wasn't looking forward to being a new kid in school again, being unchosen for teams until the very end, standing at the side pretending I wasn't interested in playing.

I hoped Bonnie wouldn't get hurt by the world's indifference.

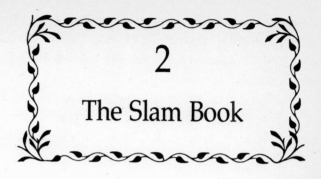

2

The Slam Book

Grade six. I thought, somehow, it would be different. My last year in elementary school. Our teacher, Mr. Johns, made a speech to the class about how tough this year would be.

I looked around at my classmates. They all seemed so big and aloof. Occupying the back desks were the big boys, their long legs and huge feet sticking out into the aisles, their eyes cast downward at their desks, their hands fumbling with pens. One was drawing on his hand while another systematically ran his ballpoint pen down a groove in the desk. Some even had fine peach-fuzz glistening on their cheeks. One glanced up at me and stared, then winked. I dropped my eyes and turned my attention back to Mr. Johns.

"There are many new students with us this year," our teacher was saying, "and it's up to the local students to make them feel welcome." I heard a snicker. "We can all learn from others. One of our new students is from Australia. I am sure she will have many interesting stories to share with us. Another is a new Canadian of East Indian extraction. I expect you to help her learn our language and our customs."

"What next," one boy muttered from the back.

"Our town has experienced exceptional growth during the past two years," Mr. Johns went on. "Our new packing plant is attracting workers . . . "

"Bums."

My back went rigid.

" . . . as well as our oil industry. Do you know we have three thousand gas and oil wells within a 21-mile radius of Gardin? New subdivisions have been built and our facilities are being upgraded to handle the growing population."

I heard a movement at the back and before I could turn around a voice boomed out. "You can say what you want, Mr. Johns, but I ain't buyin' it. We were ranchers here since this land was settled and I don't have to go welcoming all the creeps and bums who decide to settle here and work the oil patch. Or the bloody packing plant."

A chorus of agreement followed. Mr. Johns' lips tightened. "Thank you, Jim. That's the beauty of this country. We can all enjoy freedom of expression. We will debate this matter further in our Social Studies. In the meantime, however, I want you to display good manners. Our grade six class can be a model of democracy. Agreed?"

"Bull."

Mr. Johns strode down the aisle, his suit coat

flapping as he rushed past me to confront the of-fender. It wasn't Jim, but another boy, just as big with long dark hair and eyes like grey slate. "Ber-nard, I will not have that language in my class. You are here to learn tolerance and understanding. It will serve you well when you are an independent adult. I demand an immediate apology for your behaviour."

The air stilled. I looked at the boy sitting across from me and our eyes held, then we both looked away, embarrassed.

"Yeah, yeah."

"That is not an apology. And please stand up when you address me."

The boy, whose name I later discovered to be Bernard Bazant, moved his big body sideways, crablike, out of the desk, and slowly unfolded to his full height. He stood an inch taller than Mr. Johns. He looked down at the teacher, his grey eyes nar-rowing slightly. "Sorry."

"*Mr.* Johns."

"Mr. Johns."

"All right." Mr. Johns turned sharply and strode to the front. "I will be keeping a close eye on this class. You are bright kids. Your world is changing. You can grow with the changes, or allow them to beat you down. I am here to see that you have positive experiences."

"They think we're trash," the boy across from me whispered after Mr. Johns had excused us for the day. "My name is Jamie Butterick. My dad works at the plant."

"Mine does too. I'm Sherri Farquhar."

We walked out together and stood uncertainly in the hallway. Kids pushed past us, in groups. It seemed most of them knew each other, but a few kids looked kind of lost. I noted several East Indian kids, one black boy, and a number of Canadian Indians. Big farm boys pushed each other around, showing their new muscles strengthened from a summer of branding, haying, riding horseback over the range. I looked at Jamie. He was a bit shorter than me with a pinched face and long dark hair. He had blue eyes that reminded me of the bachelor-buttons that grew in Grandma's garden, a kind of deep royal blue with flecks of black.

"Do you want to go downtown?" Jamie said shyly. He rustled his book-list, clenched in his hand. "I guess we have to get this stuff today."

"Sure." Then I remembered. "Oh, I've got to wait for my little sister. She should be getting out now. She's in grade one. Do you mind if she comes with us? I'm kinda responsible for her."

"No, no problem! Let's get her."

We wandered over to another building on the school yard that housed the grades one to three classes, and stood waiting outside the door.

"You just move here?"

"Yeah, in July," Jamie said. "I took swimming this summer. Didn't meet anybody, though. I don't know . . . this seems like a kind of funny place."

"You lived in many other places?"

Jamie laughed, although it wasn't a real laugh, more of a pained exhalation of air. "Oh yeah. You hear that song, *I've Been Everywhere*? That's me. My old man's a rover. We just follow the sun."

"Us too. I went to three schools this year. Counting from January first. We were in Calgary, then in February we moved to Regina."

"Regina . . . in February? You musta been crazy. That's the coldest place in the world . . . except for Winnipeg and Wawa."

I laughed. "Wawa? Where's that?"

"Ontario. Dad worked there in the steel mill . . . for a while. It's cut records for the coldest weather. And then there's the Yukon. You ever lived up there?"

"No."

"I have. I was born there, in Whitehorse."

"That's a neat name."

"Yeah. I liked the north. But . . . construction's done there so we came south. To this place in the middle of nowhere."

Bonnie's class came pouring out then and her excitement from her first day of school carried us into a high mood.

As Mom would be taking Bonnie and me shopping in the afternoon, we just went along with Jamie while he bought pencil crayons, a geometry set, binders and paper. Then we went and had a coke float in the New World Cafe.

Bernard and his gang were piled into a back booth, being loud and throwing stuff around, but they didn't recognize us; if they did, they didn't let on, even when they left their booth and sauntered past. Bernard let his finger trail along our table, and

I heard Jamie suck in his breath as if trying to make no sound that would attract Bernard's attention. Bernard's finger was almost the size of Jamie's wrist.

Dad occasionally brought someone home from the plant for coffee or arranged an evening out with another couple to try to help Mom get to know people. So far these evenings had been disastrous. Mom was afraid to leave Bonnie and me home alone, even though at twelve I was old enough to babysit. We knew the neighbours on the other side of our duplex, and I assured Mom I could run over there in case of emergency. The men occupying the duplex facing our door didn't bother her too much; they seemed to stick to themselves, and that's the way Mom wanted it.

One night after Mom and Dad had come home from having dinner at a local hotel cabaret, I awoke to sounds of Mom crying in the kitchen. I leaned over in bed and looked at my alarm clock: twelve midnight. What was wrong? I crept out of bed and, wrapped in an afghan, crouched down behind my partly closed bedroom door.

"I can't bear it, Bill. I just can't."

"It's not my fault, Pauline. I didn't know it would be like that. We won't go there again. Bunch of cavemen. That's all they are."

"We could have been killed!"

"Nah, they just go at each other. You're safe enough. They wouldn't harm you."

"They're savages!" Mom cried. "Crazy with drink and goodness knows what else. From now on I'll only go to the Legion. It's the only safe place in this town."

I crept out into the hall.

"Mom?"

"Sherri! What are you doing up?"

"I heard you talking." I went over to her and she put out her arms. I lay my head against her soft velvet sweater. She stunk of old cigarette smoke. "Where were you?"

"Daddy and I went out to what we thought was a nice place, in a hotel cabaret where you can have supper and dance. Hah!" She was silent a moment. Her hand absently brushed my hair over my eyes, just like she did with the dog, until static electricity formed, making me itch. The smell of stale smoke was smothering.

I lifted my head. "What happened?"

"Nothing, dear. Nothing. I just didn't like it, that's all."

Dad, sitting down at the table, looked suddenly old. His hair was mussed and I could see his scalp showing through at the top where the bright kitchen light shone down. My dad was turning bald! He rubbed his hands over his face. "There's good places and bad, Sherri. It seems we went to the wrong place. Now you go to bed, that's a good girl. We'll see you in the morning."

By overhearing conversations I pieced together what had happened. Dad had gone to the bathroom and just as he was going in, a man came staggering out gasping like he was going to die. It turned out some stupid guy had taken a container of sulphuric acid and thrown it all over the sinks.

The next day I looked up "sulphuric acid" in a science book at school. H_2SO_4. A heavy, colourless, oily, very strong acid. Used in making explosives, in refining petroleum, etc.

School was a bit of a war zone too. Gangs dared each other to cross territorial lines on the playground. I hated lunch hours and recesses. At first some of us tried to stay in, but the teachers said it was healthy to go outside.

The first time the Slam Book was passed to me I didn't know what it was. Covered in a bright-green binder, the inside page said simply, "SLAM BOOK." I had noticed it being passed down the aisle during the past week, but no one said anything about it. On page one I read: "Everyone who writes in this book is sworn to an oath of secrecy. Anyone caught showing this book to a person outside this room (especially Parents or Teachers!!) will meet an early death! This is a Truth Book. Get rid of your bitches here!"

The next five pages were filled with comments against every race, religion and lifestyle to be found in our classroom, as if the world's basic problems could be exposed within these covers. It was an interesting idea.

I took the book home and, after supper, curled up

on my bed to read it. After half an hour I discovered
the flow of anger that existed in my school:

The Indian kids in my school were resentful of
the white ranchers who had invaded their territory.
The ranchers' kids hated the farmers who had
fenced off the land and ploughed it up, causing
erosion. Everyone blamed everyone else for the
death of the buffalo, antelope, pheasants, etc.
which were once here in abundance. People who
worked in industry came, building "black smoke
stacks" (I have yet to see any of these in Gardin).
These "creeps" were hated by everyone who had
been here before them. As the last group included
us, I took special note. Then I wrote in the Slam
Book:

"My family and I moved to Gardin because of a
job in the new packing plant. It is a good job for my
father, and we want to be good citizens of the
community. My father has grade 12, and so does
my mother. The only thing not pure in our family is
our dog, and we took him in as an act of charity. We
give to the Red Cross and the Salvation Army. I
have nothing against people of another country or
lifestyle as long as they learn to speak English and
are nice. I will write about them in Social Studies
essays. I will not tolerate local kids throwing their
weight around, and if they continue to pick on
people new to the town, I will write to the news-
paper."

I didn't sign my name. No one did in the Slam
Book. That way you could say what you liked and

get it off your chest. I took the book back the next day and passed it on to Jamie.

"I can't write in this, Sherri," Jamie whispered, his eyes darting down as he shoved the book back into my hands. The way he avoided looking at people was beginning to bug me. And he whispered so much of the time. Jamie had better be careful, I thought, or he would be called a wimp, and nothing could help him then. A girl sticking up for a wimp would make his life even worse.

The Slam Book came to a sudden end the week after I made my entry. The mayor's daughter Jeanne took it home and showed it to her mother, who could not be made to understand that this was a release of tensions, not a cause. She promptly brought it to the attention of the school board, and Mr. Johns was called up to explain it. We heard he tried to defend the idea, saying that knowledge of problems was the first step in solving them, but the school board banned the Slam Book and put Mr. Johns on review.

He tried to explain it to the class. Bernard and Jim and the rest of the local people sat in silence, looking as if this didn't concern them at all. But it did. It concerned all of us.

3

Scarface

When school started we forgot about our new neighbours. Occasionally we would see them drive up in their mud-spattered pickup and enter the house, letting the aluminum door slam behind them. At times a different man would stay for a few days until we weren't sure who really lived there. None of the men spoke to us, even when we were standing on the sidewalk outside their door. We got used to having them ignore us, and decided we preferred it.

That all changed the day Scarface moved in.

My sister and I were standing at the front window, looking out onto the dusty street and half-built apartment building across from us, when a Ford pickup careened down the street and spun a U-turn at our front door. It screeched to a stop in front of the next-door duplex. A man jumped out, disappearing momentarily in the cloud of dust he had created, then strode around the front of the truck. Bonnie gasped and I felt myself shudder.

The man was small-built with long dark hair matted in strands. His thick black eyebrows joined in the middle, shading ice-grey eyes. But his face . . . oh, his poor face. A scar ran from the outer tip of his right eyebrow down his cheek, between his nose and his lip, and onto his left jaw.

Worse, the stitches were still in it. The scar was red and oozing blood, like a curving red-and-black caterpillar crawling across his face.

He glanced up at the window and tipped his fingers to the side of his beaked cap in a kind of salute. I touched my fingers to the window in a feeble wave, then drew Bonnie back. We went to our room quietly, saying nothing about the man.

We saw him often during the next few weeks. "They work on an oil rig," Dad told us, "out on the rig for ten days and home for ten days. We won't see much of them."

On Scarface's days off he worked on a Ford Bronco that he had towed up to the back of their duplex, just a few feet from our door. He always whistled through his teeth while he worked on the motor. "Hi," he said when we came by, and we would mumble "Hi" to be polite, then hurry inside.

When Dad told us the company was having a picnic to celebrate the opening of the packing plant, we could hardly wait. It was to be held at the feed lot across the highway from the plant. In the early afternoon of a bright blue September day we piled into the station wagon, ignoring the dog's pleas to be included, refusing to watch his pointed brown fox-face peering at us from between the curtains as we drove away.

At the feed lot, cowboys and Indians wandered about, introducing their wives to their bosses or clustering in groups to visit. A few of the cowboys were riding horses. "They work for us herding cattle," Dad said. "The others work inside the plant doing just about anything."

A sign said tours of the packing plant were being offered. "Can we go in?" Bonnie asked.

"No, better not," Dad said. "You'll see things you shouldn't."

"Come on," I said to Bonnie, suddenly wise. "Let's go visit the cows in the corral."

We walked over to see Jamie sitting up on the fence, looking down at the white-faced cattle milling around the corral. We leaned against the boards and petted the cattle in the middle of their foreheads where the hair swirled every which way. Looking into their eyes was like peering into deep pools, trying to imagine the secret life that swam beneath the glassy surface.

"They're nice," Bonnie said, looking up at Jamie for confirmation.

"Naw, they're dumb as stumps," Jamie said. He looked angry. His lips were thin and his upper lip twisted up in a kind of sneer. It made me not want to be around him.

"Anything the matter?" I asked. After all, I was his friend – his only friend. He could tell me.

"No, everything's perfect." He threw a bunch of dried grass onto the back of one of the cattle, where it rode like a bird's nest. Bonnie laughed to see the cow nonchalantly walk around, unaware of the small burden Jamie had thrust upon it.

"Everything's just perfect," Jamie said again, and a shudder ran through me at the sad coldness of his voice. Then I looked over near the silos and I saw Jamie's dad leaning against one of the loaders. Blood was running from his nose. Two men were holding him back. Walking away from him was Mr. Munch, the foreman of the Kill Floor, looking black and angry as a prairie tornado. "Drunk," Jamie said. Then, before I could say anything, he slid off the fence and went walking through the manure-sodden corral, bravely daring one of the cattle to charge him, to give him a reason for his hurt.

We were called to eat, and sat at picnic tables (planks held up by saw-horses with oilcloths stapled over top) munching beefburgers. We looked back at the cows, who stared at us. Above our heads an electronic fly killer sputtered each time a fly came into contact with its deadly blue rays.

It was October now, and the days were getting shorter.

"Soon we'll be walking home from school in the dark," I told Bonnie authoritatively, "so you'd better get used to getting home by yourself. I won't be around every day to walk you."

"Where will you be, Sherri?" she asked timidly, and I suddenly hated myself for creating the look of fear in her eyes.

"Things start happening when you're in grade six. Maybe I'll join a club or something. Take figure skating."

"I could take figure skating too."

I stopped in the middle of the path. We had to first cross the school yard, a big empty expanse of scrubby lawn cornered with ball diamonds backed by high chicken-wire backstops, go two blocks through a subdivision, then through an empty lot. The lot was high with weeds and littered with chunks of concrete dumped from some old construction job. In the summer it had been alive with squeaks of gophers, grasshoppers and singing birds. Now it was brown and quiet, as if a blanket had been pulled over the layer of summer life.

"You can't do everything I do," I said, planting my feet on the path so Bonnie couldn't pass. "It's time you got your own friends. I'll be a teenager soon. I can't always be looking after you."

"I know." Bonnie stopped, her eyes on the dirt path. She scuffed her toe against an imbedded rock. "Can I come with you for Halloween?" Her whispered words were almost drowned by the sudden sharp caw of a crow.

"Mom says we can't go trick-or-treating this year," I said. "Not here. She doesn't like the people. She doesn't trust them."

"Why?"

I turned and started walking again. "She thinks they're the kind to put pins in apples, or razor blades in popcorn balls."

Bonnie trailed behind, banging her plastic lunch kit against her knees as she walked. It would be beyond Bonnie's imagination to believe people would do such things.

I knew a lot of things Bonnie didn't. I knew Dad wasn't happy working at the packing plant. At first he said it was the best job he'd ever had, but soon after that the problems started.

"The vans are never there when it's time to load," he'd grumble. "Men couldn't care less about showing up. We have to hire every bum who crawls up the driveway." It sounded to me just like other jobs Dad had had. They were always good at first too.

It got so I could count on one complaining session with every meal. Bonnie and I just stayed quiet and let him run down everybody and everything at the plant, while Mom murmured, "Um hum . . . pass the butter, please," and gave us little secret looks, rolling her eyes and almost causing us to laugh out loud. But it made me sad too, because I remembered going through this before, and it always ended with us packing up and moving on.

Dad occasionally brought home other men who worked at the packing plant. Mr. Munch and his family lived down the street from us in a duplex exactly like ours. He was a big man, like my dad, but looked something like a Munster with a head as big as an old tree stump and hollow dark-ringed eyes.

One day Mr. Munch came to return one of our kitchen knives that Dad had asked him to sharpen. "Test that!" he said proudly, running his thumb over the sharp edge of the blade, then holding it out toward Mom. She gingerly took the knife by its handle and placed it on the counter. "Thank you," she mumbled. Her hand shook as she let go of the knife handle.

Mr. Munch stood by the door, his big hand covering the lock. "Well, I better keep going," he said. "I bought fifty chickens from the Hutterites. We're butchering them in the basement."

"The basement!" Mom cried. "You're butchering them in the *basement*?"

"Yeah, me and the wife got it all set up. Come on down if you want. You can have one or two if you pluck 'em."

After he left, Mom sat on the chesterfield for a long time, rocking in time to some silent music inside her head, and staring out through the dust-coated living-room window.

One night when we got home from school, Scarface had a surprise: two little pups. "Oh!" Bonnie exclaimed when she saw them, and the man turned around. He neither smiled nor frowned, so we edged forward. The pups ran to us, balls of light-grey fuzz.

"What kind are they?" I asked.

"Came from a husky bitch. Likely some German shepherd in 'em somewhere."

"Can we play with them?"

Scarface looked back at the motor of the Bronco, then down at the pups. "We'll be using them out in the bush," he said curtly. "They ain't pets."

Bonnie continued to play with the shy pup who had crept up to her only after the brave one had made sure we were friendly. She put her face down onto its fuzzy head. "How old are they?" she asked timidly.

"Four, five months," he said, his head under the hood of the Bronco. He was beginning to sound annoyed.

I drew Bonnie up. "Thanks for letting us play with your pups," I said, but he must not have heard me.

The next night the pups were chained to the axle of the Bronco.

"How can they do that?" I asked Dad. He sat in a kitchen chair, running his hands over his face.

"They'll do what they darn well please around here," he muttered. "There's no law says they can't." He rubbed his red eyes.

"But it's mean!"

"Nobody said life was easy, honey," he said softly, staring into his coffee cup.

I went to my bedroom and climbed up on the bed so I could look out on the pups. They sat, buffeted by the wind that whipped around the duplexes, staring into their dishes.

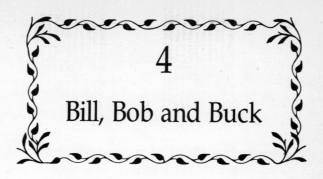

4

Bill, Bob and Buck

In some ways the discovery of the Slam Book calmed things down for a while. I now had two friends: Jamie Butterick, and Lori Swenson who lived on a ranch.

Lori and I were assigned to work on a science project together, and we decided to do studies of life forms that had once existed on the prairies. Perhaps we would find relics of old Indian arrowheads or primitive tools.

"Why don't you spend the weekend with me, Sherri?" Lori invited. "We could ride over to the coulee and see the Indian writing on the stone cliffs. We could take pictures. That should get us a good mark."

The Swenson ranch had been homesteaded by Lori's great-grandparents, one of the first ranching families in the district. Her great-grandfather, Lori told me, had come to Canada on a cattle drive from Montana with Tom Lynch in 1882. He worked around ranches near High River, Alberta, in the foothills of the Rocky Mountains. Then in 1900 he had established this cattle ranch north-west of Gardin, with six hundred cattle, a string of horses and some ranch equipment.

I envied the history behind their name. When you said "the Swenson place," everyone knew where it was.

Their house had been added onto so many times that the rooms were like extensions of the family. The kitchen and living room were all that remained of the first house where her great-grandparents had lived. An upstairs had been added and a verandah and two bedrooms off the main floor. It was big and cool in the summer, shaded by the vine-covered verandah, and cozy and warm in the winter, heated by a big wood stove in the kitchen. A bushy caragana hedge surrounded the yard where Mrs. Swenson's pink peonies and blue foxglove came up every spring, as faithful as the people who had planted them.

Lori was always laughing. She had strong white teeth the same as her dad, and big blue eyes like her Swedish mom. Lori had been riding horses all her life. She entered gymkhana competitions and showed me ribbons she'd won for barrels, poles and quarter-mile races. She demonstrated on her horse, Duchess, how barrel races were run in a clover-leaf pattern around three large drums set up in the corral. Lori's short brown hair flew up in curls from beneath her felt cowboy hat, making her look like a happy elf as she guided Duchess on ever-narrowing circles around the barrels.

The Swensons employed three full-time cowboys: Bill, Bob and Buck. I laughed when Lori recited their names, predictable names as flat and old as the prairies. Bill and Bob were brothers and were old bachelors. Their faces were windburnt and brown but unlined; the only wrinkles were around their eyes, which Bill called "ghosts of smiles."

On Friday night we sat around the big ranch table, eating a supper that tasted so delicious I thought I'd never stop. There was a huge casserole of scalloped potatoes, slices of ham baked with brown sugar and cloves, peas and carrots shining with butter and salt and pepper, canned red tomatoes that came right from the Swensons' summer garden, home-baked bread still steaming from the oven. Then two kinds of pie, apple and blueberry, topped with ice cream. The table had a revolving "lazy Susan" in the middle so the big bowls of food could make the circle without burning your hands passing them on.

After supper the men stayed, smoking "roll-yer-owns" while Mrs. Swenson, Lori and I cleared the table. "Just stack the dishes," Mrs. Swenson said. "Let's sit down and have our coffee first."

Coffee? I had never been offered coffee at home. After dinner Mom would clear the table and Bonnie and I do dishes while Mom and Dad had their coffee in the front room. I helped myself to the sugar and farm cream, adding liberal doses of both to my coffee, and leaned back to listen to the conversation.

They had just finished fall branding of the calves that had been born too late for spring branding. It had been a good year for hay; the big round bales were laid out neatly like long rows of pipe. Bill and Bob were going to ride the fences tomorrow, to fix any that were down before the snow came.

"Have to wait till after eight to go out," Bob drawled. "Early mornings it's so dark you have to use a black cat for a lantern." He looked over at me to see how I was accepting his tall tales. I grinned at him and he winked, then reached into his shirt pocket and extracted a round can of Copenhagen snuff. Pinching off a bit, he offered me the can.

"No, thanks. I'm trying to quit."

He looked at me for a moment, then threw his head back and laughed. Bill smiled shyly, his blue eyes twinkling.

I learned not to stand downwind of Bill and Bob when they chewed snuff outside. Like the grasshoppers that clicked in the prairie grass, they shot the chewed brown snuff out at regular intervals, not caring where it landed. In the house they were more polite, making trips out the back door to spit it over the verandah railing onto the frozen remains of Mrs. Swenson's flowerbeds.

Buck was the gentleman of the three. He was in his twenties, much younger than Bill and Bob, and was good looking with thick black hair and soft hazel eyes. He smoked only "roll-yer-owns," which he could roll in one hand while riding his horse.

"If I was older, Buck would be my boyfriend," Lori told me later when we were upstairs in bed, under her big down comforter. "I dream about him sometimes. I pretend I'm the same age as my sister Jennie. She got married last fall. Buck was in love with her, but he never said so, so she married Jake Bowman, who runs the farm implement place in town." She leaned over and whispered in my ear: "Buck has a broken heart."

The next day we saddled up the horses; Lori rode Duchess and gave me a little brown mare named Flame. Then she showed me how to get the bit into Flame's mouth and slip the bridle up over her ears. I was shaking with excitement. The only time I'd ever ridden a horse was on Grandpa's friend's farm, when I had been allowed to ride a big old work-horse around the farmyard with Grandpa leading him. Lori saddled Flame, showing me how to tighten the cinch by giving Flame a knee-kick in the belly to get the air out of her. "They blow themselves up," she said. "Look." And she tightened the cinch another three inches.

We started down a trail leading to the coulee, a deep ravine that dropped down into a narrow river valley, Lori and Duchess in front, me and Flame following. "Duchess is a natural leader," Lori explained. "She won't tolerate any other horse in front of her."

As we talked, I watched Flame's ears flick back and forth, as if she were listening to our conversation. I leaned over and patted her neck. Her fur was beginning to thicken up for winter, but the new hair was soft to the touch. Her black mane and tail flipped with the wind, and to me she was the heroine of every horse book I'd ever read.

A hawk slowly swooped down into the valley. We heard a squawk, and the hawk soared up with something imprisoned in its beak. The prairie sky seemed to close us in, like the top of a blue eggshell. The October sun shone down, warming our backs.

After a half-hour's ride we came to the coulee. Lori dismounted, throwing the reins onto the ground. I slowly slid down, my legs stiff and wobbly from their unaccustomed position in the saddle. "You'll have to hobble Flame," Lori said. "She won't stay." She drew from her saddle bag a small piece of rope with straps at either end, then leaned down and buckled the loops above Flame's front hoofs. "There. Now we can go explore the cliffs."

We picked our way through rock formations that rose in majestic crags over the valley. The wind, which had whipped along over the flat plains, was suddenly stilled behind the cliff, and the noises of the prairie came softly: the rustle of a small animal – a mouse perhaps? – the long caw of a crow, the whinny of one of the horses.

Lori and I sat down on a rock ledge.

"Look," she said, pointing to a rock face protected by an overhanging shelf. There, reflecting in the afternoon sun, were blood red outlines of strange pictures and signs.

"These were painted by Indians over a hundred years ago," Lori said. "Nobody touches them here. Tourists don't know about them. In the badlands along the Red Deer River there were some, but people marked them up, tried to scrape them off. You know . . . people."

I tenderly touched one of the marks. The red ochre drawings of a sun, a horse and a man wearing a big headdress felt warm.

"Jamie told me he has seen pictographs like this in Ontario at Lake Superior Provincial Park near Wawa," I said. "I never thought I'd see some with my own eyes."

Lori took a camera from her packsack and snapped two pictures of the Indian writing. "Let's not identify where it is," she said. "It's up to us to protect it."

I suddenly felt important, a protector of Western Canadian history. Maybe we would stay here, in Gardin, and the Farquhar name would become part of its past. Maybe.

We walked past high boulder formations down to the valley's basin.

"This is where one of the first police arrests were made," Lori said. "I think they were called the Northwest Mounted Police then. They arrested a man for running a still. See, he got his water from the creek there, it's pure spring water."

We knelt down at the creek and cupped the water in our hands. It was clear and icy. I touched my lips to it and immediately they felt stiff with cold. "It's delicious," Lori said. "Must have made great whisky." We laughed and sipped from the cold sweetness.

We arrived back at the ranch in the late afternoon

as the sun was falling toward the horizon. As we neared the yard we saw Buck ride in from the opposite direction. A bawling cow was running along behind him, and we could see Buck carried something on the saddle. "Buck's found a calf," Lori said, urging her horse into a lope. I kicked Flame into a jagged trot.

"Thought the little beggar was dead," Buck said, sliding down from his long-legged black horse. "Born down in the gully there. Puny little thing." He gently lifted the calf down, then, taking off his mackinaw jacket, he began to rub it vigorously. It wobbled about on its scrawny legs as the bawling mother cow nosed his arm. "It's okay, Mama, she's gonna be all right," Buck crooned to the anxious cow. "She's gonna be just fine. You gotta take better care of her, is all. Here, we'll put you both in the corral for a couple of days. Okay?"

Buck looked up from the tousled calf and grinned, holding his mackinaw toward me in out-stretched hands. "Come here, let me fix your hair with this. Works good, don't you think?" He laughed, his white teeth flashing.

I think I would be in love with him too, if I were as old as Jennie.

5

Jamie

Jamie Butterick lived in a blue trailer in a shabby cramped trailer park on the north end of town. The Buttericks' trailer was small and old and smelled like they didn't empty the garbage very often.

Jamie had no brothers or sisters that he knew. His father had been married twice before and had lost track of kids he'd had with his other wives.

"Don't you ever wonder about your half-brothers or sisters?" I asked him.

We were sitting in the vacant lot on pieces of broken concrete. I watched Bonnie carefully riding her two-wheel bike up and down the path. She had just inherited my old bike, and wasn't allowed to ride it on the road.

"Sure, I guess so," Jamie replied. "I don't think of it very often. I'll never see them anyway. They are way up north somewhere."

"But what about when you're grown up and maybe you go up there to work," I persisted.

Jamie shrugged. "I don't need them." His thin shoulders looked unnaturally puffed in the big nylon down-filled jacket his mother had bought him for winter. It was at least one size too big.

Jamie was having a difficult time at school. He was picked on, maybe because he was small and was no good at sports, a necessity for a guy to be accepted in this school, or maybe because he moved so often he had no self-confidence to try to learn games. That happens when you're scared: you're done for. It's the same whether you deal with animals or people, Lori told me. If a horse or a dog knows you're scared, they take advantage. Fear keeps you running forever.

Jamie had been beaten up twice this fall when he was walking home from school. Some big boys had formed around him, teased him, slapped him around, gave him a bleeding nose. He was never hurt too badly, but he became quieter and quieter until he was even being picked on by the teacher for never speaking up in class. His report card, which he hid in an inner pocket of his down jacket, was mostly fail marks. He had been afraid to show it to his parents.

Bonnie wobbled toward us on her bike, her blond hair fluffed out from beneath her toque. "I can ride, Jamie! See?"

He looked up and smiled. Jamie had nice teeth, that's one thing he had going for him. He would be a good-looking man some day, I thought, if he could get rid of that scared-rabbit look. Jamie was alone a lot. His mother worked as a waitress in the Dome Hotel, and was usually going on shift at four o'clock when we stopped in at Jamie's place after school.

We started down the path, Bonnie riding beside us on the grass. As we approached his trailer, his mother met us at the door.

"I wouldn't go in there right now," she said. "Bring your friends home another time."

"Why?" Jamie asked. "I invited Sherri and Bonnie in to see my hamsters."

"No, I don't think so," his mother said. "Some other time. That stupid jerk. I think sometimes he's gone off his rocker."

I looked over at Jamie and I could see a corner of his eye twitch, as it did when he was nervous.

"Can they just come in for a minute?" he asked.

His mother glanced at her watch and looked anxiously down the road. I knew she had to be on shift at four o'clock, and she was already late.

"Well, I may as well warn you," she said at last, impatient to get going, "your dad's into the sauce again."

I could see Jamie's right eye jump, then squeeze shut.

"Why?" he whispered. "He was supposed to quit."

I turned around. Bonnie was staring wide-eyed from Jamie to Mrs. Butterick.

Mrs. Butterick impatiently shifted from one foot to the other, sticking out her right hip. She dug a cigarette from a package in her purse, lit it, and threw the match over the steps to die in the gravel.

"Well, who knows why," she said. "Why do men do anything?"

Jamie's mother impatiently threw the cigarette onto the gravel. I watched it glow amid the dirt and small stones until it too died. "I've got to get to work. If he gets bad, come down to the hotel for your supper later."

Jamie watched her start the car and back down the driveway. He turned to us. "Want to see the hamsters?"

I felt nervous but curious. "Sure." I turned back to Bonnie. "You wait here," I said, and followed Jamie inside.

It took a minute for my eyes to adjust, but only a second for me to see the room. It was in shambles. Jamie's father slumped bare-chested on the couch, his big beer gut hanging over his pants. His eyes were turned inward as if he was half-asleep. The smell of smoke and beer and a sweaty body caused my breath to stop in shock after the crisp coldness of the outside air. Mr. Butterick sat up suddenly, staring at us.

"What do *you* want?" he said in a belligerent tone. "What are you doing sneaking around?"

"I just brought my friend here to see the hamsters," Jamie said in a whispery voice.

"What? Can't hear you, talk like a mouse. Thought I wasn't going to be home, didn't you? Sneaking people in when no one's home. Who do you think you are?"

He tried to stand but fell back against the couch, muttering to himself.

I stumbled outside, falling over the steps, and ran down the gravel path. I heard Bonnie call "Sherri! Wait!" but I didn't turn around. I ran until I reached the open lot and sat once again on an abandoned chunk of concrete. Bonnie came panting up on her bike and, suddenly grown-up for her age, sat in silence on another concrete slab.

I put my face into my hands and tried to block out the sight of Jamie's father. I recalled the first time I had met Mr. Butterick.

"Yeah, I know your old man, Bill Farquhar," he had said. "Shipping foreman. Good guy." He burped and took another slug of beer, then turned back to watching the football game on television.

"What do you do at the plant, Mr. Butterick?" I had asked to be polite.

He looked at me vaguely as if trying to remember. Then he grinned, showing a straight row of yellow teeth. "I slit throats and skin heads," he said.

I sat on the concrete until the penetrating pain of coldness forced me to start walking slowly homeward. Bonnie silently followed, pushing her bike. I could hear her breath in the cold crisp autumn air, coming in rasps that sounded like the panting of a little animal.

6
Halloween Tricks and Treats

Halloween parties took the gloom off the cold grey autumn days.

Our grade six class was asked to organize the party for all three grade six classes, and I was chosen to be on the decorations committee. We were holding the party in our classroom, and for the afternoon all the desks were being carried across the hall and stored in another room. We had a tape player and music so we could dance, although I couldn't imagine grade six boys asking girls to dance. The image of Bernard or Jim dancing caused me to giggle. My decorating partner, Mary-Ann Murphy, looked at me quizzically.

"I'm just trying to imagine these big oafs in our class dancing," I said.

She laughed. "You haven't been around here very long, have you?"

"No, we moved in August. Why?"

"You're in for a surprise. These ranch boys have

been going to dances since they were babies in blankets. You've never been to a country dance?"

"No."

"Poor deprived city girl." She sighed with mock despair. "You should get your parents to take you to one. They're a blast."

I continued twisting the black-and-orange streamers. Lori Swenson often mentioned country dances, and I had wondered how she had been able to describe them so well. I couldn't imagine my parents taking Bonnie or me to a dance.

"There's a dance out at Furness on Saturday night," Mary-Ann continued. "You should get your parents to buy tickets. Then you and your little sister would get a real view of this place."

We taped the streamers corner-to-corner across the room and hung black paper witches and orange pumpkins from the crosspiece. Paper ghosts were stuck onto windows and blackboards, and we even made a display in one corner with real stooks of grain and three big pumpkins, which were to be raffled off for jack-o'-lanterns after the party. Prizes of pens and notepads and coloured felt markers (provided by the school) would be given for the best jack-o'-lantern from each class, best costume in categories of horror, humour and how well the costume hid the identity of the person.

Country kids who came in by bus brought their costumes in bags and changed in the washrooms at noon. Bonnie and I went home for lunch and Mom helped us dress and put on our make-up. Bonnie was an angel and I was a witch. Bonnie was the cutest angel. Mom applied rouge to her cheeks, make-up to her eyes and even pink lipstick to her lips. Her silver tinsel halo sparkled and bounced on its supporting wire above her head. Her long white angel gown glittered with sparkles, and her wand (do angels carry wands?) was a silver baton tipped with a big silver star.

Mom had made over my witch costume from last year, lengthening it to accommodate my now longer legs. Then she had fashioned a tall pointed hat, a wig of black wool hair, a false crooked nose of papier-mâché and a black eye-mask. My long black dress was decorated with silver occult signs (I had looked up patterns for them in a book) and even my black shoes had papier-mâché pointed toes sticking out, making my costume complete.

We walked back to school, carrying our hat and halo so the wind wouldn't whip them off. Bonnie was excited at the prospect of a party.

The first person I spotted in our classroom was Jamie, easy to recognize because he wore no costume. I walked over to him.

"I could have loaned you a sheet for a ghost outfit," I said softly. Jamie turned away. We hadn't been talking much lately. "Really, Jamie, we've got a couple of old sheets at home that Mom wouldn't have minded me cutting holes in for eyes."

"I don't need your old sheets, okay?" Jamie's face was pinched again. He turned on me, a sudden hard look in his eyes. "You're doing all right for yourself," he said, a note of bitterness in his voice he had never used before. "I saw you decorating. You're right in with the crowd, aren't you?"

"I don't know what you mean," I answered. "Mr. Johns picked one person from each row. I got picked."

"Yeah, sure. You and Mary-Ann Murphy, the doctor's daughter."

"Jamie, are you trying to accuse me of being a snob? If so, you can just forget it. I didn't know who Mary-Ann's father is, or care."

"He's our doctor," Jamie said. "He knows . . . everything."

"Everything?"

"Yeah." Jamie turned away, but not before I could see the tears well in his eyes. "Everything. Mom . . . they think Mom's got cancer. She's got to go to Calgary for tests."

"Oh, Jamie." I touched his sleeve but he withdrew as if my fingers were firesticks. "I'm sorry. I hope she'll be all right."

"Yeah, well, if she croaks I'm not staying with the old man. I'll run away. I hate him."

I couldn't keep back the tears that ran from my eyes beneath my mask. There was nothing I could say. Of course Jamie's mother couldn't have made him a costume, and it was always mothers who did that kind of thing. I thought of how I took it for granted that Mom would sew Bonnie's and my costumes, then be available at noon to help us dress and apply our make-up. I could understand Jamie's feelings toward his father. His father had humiliated him, but he was his father. And if something happened to his mother, he would have no one else.

"I must congratulate our decorating committee on the fine job they've done," Mr. Johns boomed out. "I can't recognize any of you now, of course, but you surely deserve credit."

Mr. Johns was only recognizable because of his voice: his costume was that of Porky Pig. How we laughed! And he laughed too, enjoying our fun. Almost everyone was dressed up – only Jamie and two other kids had not bothered. Then someone turned on the music and the party began.

The games committee had hung apples from a wire for the apple-biting contest. We watched, laughing, as the contestants tried to bite a chunk out of a swinging apple. Finally one of the boys with kind of buck-teeth got a bite, and everyone cheered as he accepted his prize. We had identity guessing contests, pin-the-tail-on-the-cat games, with an arch-backed paper cat taped to the wall. At the end of the game, tails sprouted from every portion of the cat, causing us to laugh and make snide comments.

I didn't win a prize in the costumes competition. The most unique was a running shoe; the funniest went to Mr. Johns in his Porky Pig suit, although he tried to say he was ineligible; and the horror went to Dracula, who had real wolf fangs. It was quite gross, actually, but I guess that's what horror means.

Jamie disappeared somewhere during the games

and I thought of going to look for him, but just after the costumes were judged, and the tape player was turned up so people could dance, I saw him shrugging into that big, down-filled jacket and slipping out the door. I tried to catch him, but by the time I had made my way through the crowd in the room, he was gone.

I turned back to watch the dancers. Everyone was dancing, the wildness of their costumes adding colour and excitement. My hand was grabbed and then I was dancing too, my pointed witch toes awkwardly moving to the music blaring from the speakers. I couldn't identify my partner other than from his comic character of Mickey Mouse, but before I could talk to him someone else had whirled me around and I was dancing with a duck. I was learning a lot about country living.

7
Country
Whoop-Up

"How late can we stay out trick-or-treating?" I asked. We stood by the door with costumes on, holding pillowcases that we hoped would soon be filled with treats.

Mom had finally given us permission to go out but she still seemed uneasy. Lori was coming with us too and then staying overnight, so she could enjoy an evening of trick-or-treating in town. She and I had hidden a bar of soap to write on windows where no one was home or where people refused to answer their door. Mom would have taken it from us had she known, but we figured it was an innocent trick that would do no lasting harm, and it was fun. Lori had also hidden a can of shaving cream.

"Bring Bonnie back before she gets too tired," Mom said. "Don't drag her all over town. She doesn't need too much."

"I can keep up!" Bonnie protested, and we smiled down at our innocent angel. She had no idea we would soon be whisking her through yards, down alleys, causing as much mischief as possible.

The night was warm and still. A full moon shone in the sky, illuminating the rows of houses and, beyond them, shining fields that flowed away from the town. A huge jackrabbit bounced past a street light and disappeared into somebody's back yard. I hoped the dogs wouldn't catch his scent.

We first called at the duplex facing ours, I pushing Lori in front to greet Scarface or whoever was living there at the moment. A man with a beer in his hand answered the door. "Hello, boys!" he said jovially.

"We're not boys!" Bonnie piped, and the man laughed.

"Of course! Not many boys are angels." He dug into an ice-cream bucket filled with little chocolate bars and dumped a handful into each of our bags. "Happy Halloween," he said.

"Thanks!" And on we went down the street. At the Munches' the door swung open before we had finished our cry of "trick or treat" and Mr. Munch stood blocking the door frame. His face broke into a laugh. "An angel, a witch and what's this . . . a cowgirl? How does a cowgirl rate such company?"

Mrs. Munch stood behind him on the landing, the little Munchkins clinging to her skirts, three boys ranging from about eighteen months to six years.

"Why aren't your boys out trick-or-treating?" I asked.

Mrs. Munch seemed to draw back. "They ain't

allowed," she said shortly. "They're going to bed right away."

"But it's only six-thirty!" Bonnie said.

I gave her a jab with my elbow.

The stories we had heard about the Munches must be true: that they put the boys to bed at six o'clock every evening. Once they had hired a baby-sitter who let them stay up until eight o'clock, thinking that was normal. One of the boys went to the window. "What's that?" he had said in a shocked voice, pointing outside. The babysitter had looked out. "What?" "That!" he said, pointing up to the moon. The babysitter told us that aluminum foil had been taped to the windows of the boys' bedroom so they would fall asleep quickly, and they had never been up past sundown. We tried to imagine never having seen the moon. Could it be true?

"The oldest one, Dickie, is in my room at school," Bonnie had told me. "He's weird. It's like he's never been around normal people."

Mrs. Munch came down the stairs to put suckers into our bags. "Two each," she said.

We thanked her, then added, "If you want the boys to go up and down the street, we'll take them."

The expression on Mrs. Munch's face grew cold and, for some reason, kind of afraid. "No," she said firmly.

"But, Mom," the oldest boy said in a whisper, tugging at her elbow. Mr. Munch turned and barked "Enough!" And it was. We quietly went down the steps, hardly breathing.

"Wow," said Lori, when we were out on the street. "What's with them?"

"I don't know," I replied. "My dad knows Mr. Munch. He works at the plant. They treat their kids like little prisoners. Come on, we've got hundreds of houses to call on. Let's go."

"People are different when you get to know more things about them, or see inside their house," Bonnie said. "We were told not to go to our teacher's house. She says her church doesn't like Halloween."

"It's pagan, that's why," Lori said.

"What's that?"

"Not Christian."

Bonnie thought about this for a moment. "Is Valentine's Day? She said we could have a party then."

"Yeah, it's named after Saint Valentine," Lori informed her. "But Remembrance Day isn't Christian, or Queen Victoria's birthday. We celebrate them. Tell her about that."

"Don't worry," I said, "it's her problem, not yours. We'll go soap her windows."

"I thought she was nice until she told us not to come to her house," Bonnie said darkly. "Now I think I don't like her. I don't want the Munches' suckers either. If their kids can't have them, I don't want them."

"Give them to me then," I said. And she did.

We reported home twice to empty our bags and start off again, convincing Mom to let Bonnie come with us to the very end. We even gave her a bar of soap so she could scribble soapy circles onto windows and wouldn't be able to tell on us for doing it. We met other kids walking in groups from house to house. Once we met some boys from our room who tried to hit us with eggs, but we ducked behind a car. When one boy came too close we let him have it with shaving cream. Halloween was so much fun.

The following night was the community dance in Furness. Mom and Dad had bought tickets, and Lori convinced them to take Bonnie and me. She was going with her parents, she said, and kids were given the run of the community hall basement while the adults danced upstairs.

We rode out to the little village in the station wagon, again dressed up in our Halloween costumes. Dad was dressed as an old Sourdough and looked so funny. He wore a ripped T-shirt that said, "The Squaws Along The Yukon Are Good Enough For Me," and underneath, "Whitehorse, Yukon Territory." It reminded me of Jamie being born there. Mom wore a long dress made from scraps of cloth she intended to use for a quilt. She looked pretty rather than ragged.

Cars were parked along every main road in Furness. We could hear music coming from the hotel bar, and as we drove past, the door opened. We could hear cowboy yells.

We parked the car as near as we could to the community hall and walked through the warm night air, following the crowd to the front door. People lined the wide porch steps, leaning back on the railing, enjoying the unusual warmth this late in the year. At Halloween the weather can be mild, like Indian summer, or we can have two feet of snow.

The hall was decorated with black and orange coloured streamers and cut-outs of cats, witches and pumpkins. A big stuffed witch riding a broomstick swung from the ceiling. Bonnie's eyes were shining, her angelic smile lighting up her sweet face. I scowled witch-like. "You better be good, little girl, or I'm gonna get you!" I gave her a poke in the ribs. Mom gave me a tight-lipped look. I was glad I wasn't going to be dancing with her.

At first we sat with Mom and Dad at a big table laden with bowls of potato chips, dip, peanuts in the shell and, for some reason, long black licorice whips. Bonnie and I both took a whip, seeing who could stuff it in the mouth faster. Again I was given a look from Mom that was meant to wither my spirit, but I ignored it. Nothing could ruin my mood on such a magic night.

"Come on, Bonnie, let's see if we know any of the kids downstairs."

"Be careful," Mom said, looking worried.

I looked at Dad. Careful? Of what?

"Have fun, kids," Dad said, giving us a wink.

I recognized two or three costumes from our school party and went over to them, clutching Bonnie by the hand. The fat lady was Rosalie Myers, and the ballet dancer Beth Freeman, both girls from my class. "Let's get a table together," Beth said, and we sat down, attacking the bowls of chips as if we had never eaten before. Beth's little brother sat with us too, and he and Bonnie started giggling over some childish thing. We ignored them and talked about our class party.

"There's someone here who's awful anxious to see you," Beth informed me in a teasing voice.

"Who?"

"You'll see," she said and nudged Rosalie.

I turned to watch some kids coming down the stairs: goblins, beggars, old men and fat women, movie stars, a figure skater, Dracula. How would I recognize anybody?

We heard a boom and the band started upstairs. Oh no, country and western music. And we'd be getting it second-hand as the sound burst from two huge speakers wired through the floor. The basement soon filled with kids who were being supervised by the community club ladies bustling about in the kitchen at the far end of the basement, getting the midnight supper ready.

I never expected the eruption of enthusiasm for dancing. The ceiling above us started to shake as we heard the rhythmic stomping of hundreds of feet, everyone up for the first dance, a rousing country tune. Stomp! Stomp! Stomp! Then the basement dance floor started to fill up. We couldn't tell if it was all girls dancing, or girl and boy partners, or what, just an ever-growing crowd of disguised dancers of all sizes and ages.

"Come on!" Beth grabbed my arm, and before I knew it, all of us from our table were up dancing, waving our arms and stamping our feet in time with the fast-paced melody, turning, whirling, my witch dress flowing out in black furls. Little Bonnie was a twirling dazzle of white and silver sparkles. Her eyes shone with excitement. Lori had arrived, and was whooping it up in her cowgirl costume on the far side of the floor.

"Hey!" One of the dancers bumped into me, yelled "Sorry!" and whirled away.

We were having fun, a room full of people who likely had grown up together, knew each other from birth, only Bonnie and I strangers; but with the Halloween costumes, no one was a stranger, or all were. We danced on, only going back to the table to gulp down a drink of fruit punch served from big gallon pails, replenished every few minutes by the ladies of the club.

"Let's go upstairs and watch the adults for a minute," Lori said. "We've got to chaperon them, you know!"

Laughing, we ran up the stairs and stood near the back, watching the silhouettes of the dancers making their musical rounds of the dance floor. I spotted Mom and Dad, dancing cheek to cheek, and pointed them out to Bonnie. She giggled behind her hand. Maybe an evening like this was just what they needed. Lori's parents, Mr. and Mrs. Swenson, had invited them to join their table, so they would be with a group, not alone.

"Can I have this dance?" I looked up to see a gorilla extending his paw. I recognized the voice. No, couldn't be. I caught Lori's eye and she gave me a knowing wink. Oh boy.

I moved out to the dance floor, turned around, and felt myself being enveloped in a gorilla hug. Only then did I realize the dance was a waltz, and I was in the hairy arms of big Bernard Bazant.

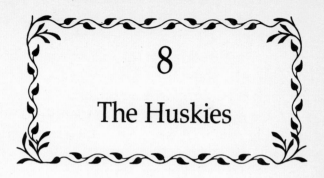

8

The Huskies

Fall passed into winter. We were spending Christmas with Grandma and Grandpa. Dad had to work until four o'clock on Christmas Eve, so we didn't get away until dark. We packed the station wagon with suitcases, presents, a big ham that tempted the dog to sniff and lick at the box when he thought no one was looking, and blankets and pillows for Bonnie and me to snuggle into in the back seat.

We lay on our backs, staring up through the curved window into the blue-black night. Two inches of new snow had fallen the day before, and the fields sparkled like Bonnie's angel gown. The moon's light silhouetted a herd of cattle standing on a ridge, giving them the appearance of a fleet of ships sailing across a rolling crystalline ocean.

Dad turned the radio on and Christmas carols filled the air. Bonnie and I sang along with the old ones, "It Came Upon a Midnight Clear," "Deck the Halls," and soon Mom and Dad were joining us. I didn't realize how well Dad could sing. His voice, loud and strong, gave the carols a sense of rightness and made me feel secure. I lay in the darkness listening to the soft sound of the snowy road whispering under the snow tires, and the sound of my Dad singing, the music drifting on, on.

I must have fallen asleep for suddenly Bonnie was shaking me, whispering, "Listen, Sherri, they've seen Santa Claus!"

"Our northern satellite system has made contact with the North Pole!" the announcer cried. "Santa and his reindeer are in the air at this minute, heading across the Yukon Territories and ... what's that? ... trouble? Rudolph's nose has lost its shine? Just one moment, boys and girls, we have an emergency here."

Bonnie gripped my arm tightly. I could feel her tension as she awaited the announcer's return after an interlude of Christmas music. I wanted to say, Don't worry, Bonnie, it will be okay, it's just a publicity gimmick, but I felt old and young at the same time. I patted Bonnie's shoulder. "Let's see if we can spot any coyotes in the fields," I said, but just then the announcer returned.

"Santa Claus has landed in Whitehorse. We've just radioed to the airport where they're standing by with a new set of batteries. Yes, he's landed, and the situation is being resolved. Rudolph's nose is again shining brightly. He'll be leading Santa and his reindeer across the Yukon and south into British Columbia ... "

"Why do they get their toys first?" Bonnie demanded, petulant now that the emergency was over.

"He has to start somewhere," I answered shortly, my interest in her thought level quickly waning. "Don't be so greedy."

She was silent then, and I lay back and stared again at the fields. We were in the ranching country of Hanna and houses were spaced several miles apart. Brightly coloured Christmas lights – some in the shape of Santa and his sleigh, some simply outlining doors and windows – gave an exciting change from the broad open fields. Christmas music came on the radio again, but I guess we were all tired for this time no one sang.

Bonnie and I got to stay at Grandma and Grandpa's over the Christmas holidays. We played with our toys, went sleigh riding down the long hill behind the house, and went skating at the arena with two girls we had met who lived there. Bonnie had been on skates since she was two years old, so I didn't have to look after her. I skated with my friends, around and around the arena, to recorded music.

I said nothing about our life in Gardin, although I wanted to tell Grandma everything – about the good things and the bad things, about my friend Lori and her ranch, and about Jamie. He had told me the last day of school that the doctor said his mother didn't have cancer, but she must have an operation and wouldn't be able to work for some time. Then his voice had dropped. "We're moving again. Down East somewhere."

"Wawa?"

He shrugged. "I don't know, maybe Churchill."
Then he turned away and that's the last I saw of
him. In some ways I felt relieved Jamie was moving.
I was glad his mother wouldn't be working. Things
might get better with her at home. Maybe.

I wanted to tell Grandma about the sulphuric
acid, about Scarface and the husky pups who
peered out at us from beneath the truck, their eyes
now sullen and hostile. I wanted to tell her I didn't
know how long we would be in Gardin, that I heard
Dad complaining more and more often about his
job, but I said nothing.

Mom and Dad came for New Year's, and took us
back.

The husky pups were now twice the size as when
Scarface first brought them home. They had shed
their fuzz and had long dark guard hairs covering
massive undercoats of lighter finer fur. They had
also shed their puppy playfulness and watched us
cautiously as we walked up our steps. Dirty circular
paths had been worn in the snow where they paced
every day, dragging chains behind them. At night
they howled, long mournful chilling cries like the
wild dogs in Jack London's stories of the North.
Bonnie and I could hear them as we lay in our beds,
and sometimes we heard answering howls from
neighbourhood dogs, or from the coyotes who
prowled on the outskirts of the Greenborough subdivision.

February and March were the coldest ever recorded in southern Alberta. Everything was rigid with ice. The dogs' dishes were frozen solid, and Bonnie and I saw them work their teeth on the plastic sides of the dishes, trying to dislodge a chunk of frozen food or lick the ice from frozen water bowls. We never spoke to the dogs anymore, and never saw the owners.

"That guy with the scars went up north for a couple of months," Dad said. "I don't think the other guys are much interested in the dogs."

"Then I'll see they don't starve," Mom said. She took to throwing them scraps, then buying big bags of dry dog food and shoving it under the Ford Bronco on the end of a shovel. We heard their chains rattle as they claimed their meagre fare. Sometimes we saw them peer out and they looked thin, even with bushy winter coats. Mom also gave them water in a bucket, bringing it inside after they had drunk.

"I don't want to interfere," she said grimly, "but I can't stand mistreating animals. Poor dumb beasts."

I didn't know if she was speaking of the dogs or their owners.

Dad was still treating us to daily reports on the situation at the packing plant.

"Never any clean laundry," he'd grumble. "Three shifts of men for two shifts of laundry. Ye gods."

"Can't you get a commercial laundry to do it faster?" Mom asked.

"You can't get *anybody* to do *anything* faster in this place," Dad said, throwing down his fork. "Nobody wants to work overtime. They're too fat, that's their problem."

Bonnie started giggling, looking down at her plate. I kicked her under the table. If she started, I'd start. Dad scraped back his chair and began pacing between the stove and the table. His hair stuck out in tufts. Grandma would have said he looked like a wild man from Borneo.

"The boss and his blasted bulls!" Dad bellowed, looking up and waving his arms to the ceiling. "All he buys is those cross-bred Charolais . . . just like bulls, all of 'em . . . quarters weigh over two hundred pounds each!"

Bonnie had lost it by this time and had to run to the bathroom where I could hear her giggles over the running water. I didn't dare look at Mom.

"And if it isn't them, it's floppy old cows. We might as well be loading wet mattresses!"

Here Mom and I let go with gales of laughter that just wouldn't quit. Dad sat down heavily in his chair, looking from one of us to the other. Then he started laughing too.

"Come here," he said. Mom and I came at him, one from each side, and just hugged him. The dog danced back and forth. Bonnie came out of the bathroom, sensing the change, and ran up to grab his knees, rolling her blond head from one knee to the other.

"Oh, my beautiful girls," Dad said. "Oh, my babies. What have I brought you to?"

I kissed the side of his head. He turned and looked at me, his brown eyes more relaxed and happy than I had seen them in quite a while.

"Now, let's finish this crazy supper," he said, picking up his fork.

March came in with howling winds straight from the North. The roads drifted over and for a while our town was isolated. The R.C.M.P. broadcast snow warnings, urging people not to travel unless it was absolutely necessary.

We tried to look under the truck to see how the dogs were doing in the cold weather, but snow and garbage had banked up around the Bronco and we were afraid to get too close to their escape hole. We hardly ever saw the guys who lived in the duplex. It sometimes seemed as if no one lived there. And then we would notice tracks showing someone had entered the house, and for some strange reason, we'd feel relief.

Dad was now working the four-to-midnight shift at the plant. The new superintendent was trying different systems, most of which didn't work. Product was shorted, quality was down, and customers were getting fed up. The manager took it out on the plant superintendent, who took it out on the shipping foreman, who was my dad. The R.C.M.P. weren't the only ones giving out storm warnings.

I awoke one night in late March to hear the wind screaming round the corner of the house. The dogs never howled anymore and sometimes I was afraid they had died, but Mom said they were still eating but not very well. I heard Dad come in, the aluminum storm door whip back, and Dad's muttered curse as he grabbed at the flimsy door before it snapped off. A sharp crack sounded, then his yelp of anger, and silence.

"What happened?" Mom was running to the door, her slippers flapping.

"Bloody thing ripped right off the door frame. Cheap junk! No good for this country. Nothing can stand up to this wind. I'll have to take the door off."

I could hear Dad outside trying to work with a screwdriver in the howling winter blizzard. The door couldn't be left hanging: it would bang all night. And it couldn't be closed.

At last Dad came in, breathing heavily, and I heard a tinny clank as he hauled the door downstairs. A loud crash told me he had hit the glass against the wrought-iron railing. I covered my head with my pillow.

Dad came upstairs and I could hear him help Mom clean up the broken glass. "Got any coffee on, Pauline?" His voice sounded tired.

"Sure."

I heard Mom go to the kitchen, the chairs scrape on the linoleum as they sat at the table.

"Should I get the liniment?" Mom asked.

"Please."

She got the bottle from the bathroom and I could hear her soothing words as she massaged his back and shoulders.

"Think I'm getting shorter, you know that,

Pauline? Loading those heavy quarters is packing down my backbone."

"Oh, come on."

"Honest."

I crept to the door, listening to see if it could really be true.

"Humping all this beef is shortening me up, Pauline. This morning I had to move the seat forward in the truck to reach the gas pedal."

"Oh, you did not!" Mom laughed and gave his shoulder a slap.

But I was scared. Dad was getting shorter. And older. The lines around his mouth hadn't been there a month ago. I was going to creep back into bed when Dad's next comment made me stand so still I could hear my heart pound in the silent dark room.

"You know, I think that dog out there's had pups," Dad said. "I could hear them whining. I'm sure of it. Check it out in the morning if you can. It's too cold for them out there."

How could they have pups? They were pups themselves! I counted: six months since Scarface had brought them home, and he had said they were around four months old then. Maybe they weren't too young . . . they just looked small because they were half starved.

"Likely some stray came around, caught her at first heat. Those guys should be hung. Dogs tied up like that. I should have let them loose long ago."

"What can we do, Bill?" Mom's voice was tight. I thought she might cry. "If this is the frontier, they can have it!" Her slippered feet slapped harshly as she went to the stove to pour more coffee. "I should have reported them to the S.P.C.A. Those dogs can't be more than a year. They're so small."

"You'd be skinny too if you just ate what a neighbour gave you on the end of a shovel."

I was leaving for school the next morning when Scarface came out of his door. I stopped dead in my tracks, shocked to see him back.

"I thought you were up north," I blurted.

He acted as if I hadn't spoken.

I clutched Bonnie's hand for security, then spoke louder. "Your dogs had pups, you know."

He suddenly seemed to find the source of my voice. "Huh?"

"Your dogs had pups. Under the truck."

"Couldn't have."

"My dad heard them. Whining."

He looked at me suspiciously. "Your dog been around them?"

"Our dog's neutered," I said. "And, anyway, he wouldn't go near your dogs. They'd kill him. They're so hungry all the time. My mom's been feeding them or they'd have died."

He jumped off the steps and knelt down in the dirty snow to peer beneath the truck. "Jesus Christ," he said. He wriggled underneath the truck and came squirming out. In his hand was a tiny white ball. "Holy Mother," he said, and crawled back under.

He came out with two more. He pulled four live

pups from under the truck as we watched, then three more, stone cold dead. He stood for a moment with the four pups squirming in his hands as if he didn't know what to do with them. I held out my mittened hands and, bewildered, he handed them to me. I gave two to Bonnie and held the other two close to my coat, trying to keep them sheltered from the wind that shrieked between our duplexes.

Scarface stood holding the three dead pups as if trying to decide what to do. Then he lifted the lid of the garbage can sitting alongside the step and shoved them inside. The garbage hadn't been emptied for months because they never hauled it to the back alley, and frozen bags were piled high against the outside wall of their duplex. The pup bodies slid down the frozen plastic onto the ground. He bent and picked them up, put them on top again and covered them gently with the lid. This time they stayed. "There," he said.

"You'd better put your dogs inside," I said, bolder now. The puppies wriggled in my hands and thrust their closed eyes toward my voice. I heard a chain rattle from beneath the truck.

"Yeah." Scarface bent to undo the chains. He had to pull hard to drag the dogs from beneath the truck. We hadn't seen them for several weeks and I was shocked into silence when they emerged, blinking, resisting the pull of the chains. Their coats were matted with dirt, their eyes darting like frightened wild things.

"Better watch out," Scarface said as he dragged them past us and through the door. The aluminum storm door shook in its frame. He booted the dogs downstairs, then came back for the pups, taking them gently from our hands.

For the next few days we saw no sign of life from next door; then on Saturday afternoon I watched at the window as one of the guys emerged from the pickup truck carrying a rifle. He reached into the box of the truck and hoisted up three frozen dead rabbits. I peered out the window in our side door to watch him enter the house and fling the rabbits downstairs.

"Surely they're not feeding frozen dead rabbits to those dogs in the basement!" Mom exclaimed. "The place will look like an abattoir."

"What's that?" Bonnie asked.

"A meat slaughtering plant."

"Like where Daddy works?"

Mom got a hard edge to her mouth. "Not quite," she said. "Almost, but not quite."

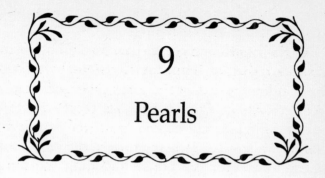

9

Pearls

One night near the end of March I awoke to hear Mom and Dad talking, the urgency in their voices causing me to come fully awake. I looked over at my lighted alarm clock. It was nearly midnight.

Although Dad was again on day shift, his unhappiness with his job remained unchanged. The tension when he was home made the air feel still.

"I don't understand the mentality around here." Dad sat in a kitchen chair. I could hear it squeak as he moved around. "They're just animals. Joe Munch told me about a stag party he went to Friday night at Fletcher's Supply Warehouse. A hundred men, a hundred bottles of booze. They ripped the hot-water tank right off the pipes. Hot water everywhere."

There was silence for a moment, then Mom spoke so low and sad I could hardly hear. "The wife of one of the R.C.M.P. constables bowls on my team. She told me there were three incidents involving guns on her street alone this past winter. A person could get shot just walking down the street! I'm afraid for the girls . . . for all of us."

"These guys make too much money, don't know what to do with it," Dad said morosely.

"Pearls before swine."

"What? Oh yeah. Maybe we're all swine, not a pearl in the whole lot."

There was silence from the kitchen and I thought Mom and Dad's conversation had ended. Then Dad spoke again, his voice sounding tired and old.

"I guess we'll have to stick it out for a while, anyway." There was a tone of despair in his statement that made me afraid, as if the future was a black hole. I dreaded moving again: new teachers, new school work, always being the new kid. I heard Dad walk over to the sink and run water into his coffee cup.

"One of the guys at the plant asked me to go snowmobiling with him this weekend. They go out in the hills, chase coyotes. Ten bucks a pelt. Just run 'em down. I told him I was busy."

"But these men make good money! Why do they have to sell coyote pelts?"

"I'll never know."

I pulled the pillow over my head, blocking out their words. I could hear Bonnie tossing about in the next room. Perhaps she had heard Dad's words, or could somehow sense the unhappiness that hung like a storm cloud. I had been excited about moving here from Regina; it was nearer to Calgary where I still had friends; it was nearer to Grandma and Grandpa. I had read books about the cowboys and Indians of the prairies and now I had even met some. I was beginning to feel at home here.

I turned over. The house was quiet now, and I could hear Mom and Dad downstairs, preparing for bed. I decided I would hate to be a grown-up.

I had matured tremendously during the six months we had been in Gardin. I had been exposed to rawness that I had never known existed. But if I had kept a diary since we moved here, it would contain more questions than answers.

I would be thirteen in July, and already I felt myself changing. My hair seemed to be coming in thicker, and Mom had taken me to a hairstylist to have it trimmed in a long blunt cut. Clothes from last winter were too short in the arms and legs. Bonnie had noticed these changes first, complaining that I never wanted to play Barbies or dress-up anymore, that I sat on my bed staring instead of playing games like I used to. "I'm not staring," I had told her, "I'm thinking."

"Well, it looks to me like you're staring," she had said, pouting. "You're getting boring."

I had turned back to the book I was reading, *Anne of Green Gables*. How she had longed for the safety and security of a home, something that most people took for granted. Sure, I had my real Mom and real Dad, which a lot of kids in my class didn't, but something was missing. We didn't come from anywhere, we weren't known anywhere. Since I was born we had lived in seven different places. Nobody remembered us. The Farquhars were not pioneers. Lori thought it exciting that I had been to four schools. She had only been to Gardin, would only ever go to Gardin until she finished grade twelve, and then maybe to the city for university or something. People like Jamie and I didn't think that far ahead. We were too busy trying to fit in where we were.

I heard Bonnie stir again, so I crept out of bed and went to her room. She seemed feverish. I soaked a washcloth in cold water, wrung it out and laid it on her hot forehead.

"I'm scared, Sherri," she kept saying over and over. "I hear the dogs."

"You can't hear the dogs," I said. "They're inside, down the basement where it's warm. They're okay."

"No, Sherri, I hear them," she said. Her eyes glowed in the dark room. "They're crying."

I sat with her a long time, until she finally fell asleep. Only then did I realize that my feet were cold and I was shivering too.

10
Ice Flowers

Bonnie and I had learned to skate when we were two years old. I guess most kids who grow up on the prairies are taught to skate almost as soon as they can walk. Dad used to flood the garden in our back yard, spraying it daily with water from the garden hose to ensure hundreds of smooth layers of ice. It took lots of work to get it started, but not much to keep it cleared off unless a warm chinook wind blew in over the Rocky Mountains and melted the top layer, leaving it honeycombed with melted spots.

We learned to skate by pushing a wooden kitchen chair along in front of us to help our balance. Then when we had the feel of the blades we tried it on our own, stumbling and falling, wobbling like baby ducks, ankles turning this way and that, until we learned to start, stop and turn, then gain speed as we circled our small rink.

I started taking figure-skating lessons three

years ago in Calgary in the outdoor rink at our community centre. We had lessons twice a week, unless the weather dropped below zero. The Ice Carnival, the final festival of our skating season, was held in a big indoor arena rented especially for that night. Our parents were invited and were asked to bring friends and neighbours to watch the performances on ice of kids from three to sixteen. I had never had a solo, or even a duet. That honour was reserved for older students who could do interesting jumps and be relied upon not to fall down after every spin.

The figure-skating classes in Gardin were really huge, as almost every girl – and half the younger boys – took part. Mothers would enroll their young boys (aged three to six) in figure skating to gain balance and skills that would be needed later for hockey.

Our teacher, Miss Wesley, was in her early twenties and very pretty. She had long dark hair that fell in waves around her shoulders, and sparkling brown eyes. As she talked she twirled around several times on her silver blades, creating showers of ice dust as she made little skid stops.

"There are forty-two different figures," Miss Wesley informed us, "and they are all based on circles. You do them on different edges of your blade and in different directions."

I looked around at the rest of my class. They appeared bored, as if they were all experts. Only the younger ones like Bonnie were listening, trying to memorize these points so they could quickly become expert skaters.

Miss Wesley started us on circles. "The diameter of your circle should be three times your body length," she said. "Balance is very important. Keep your eyes on a line about three feet in front of you. If you look down, it will throw you off." She then sent us in groups to practise circles, spirals and spread-eagles.

"I'm going to be a famous skater when I grow up," Bonnie announced on our way home. "I'll wear pretty skating outfits like Miss Wesley, and have my hair long like hers, and skate in the Ice Capades."

"I wish you luck. You'll have to practise every day for hours," I said. "Then only a small number of people are chosen for Ice Capades. Look at Miss Wesley. She must be good, yet here she is teaching in Gardin. Big thrill."

"I think she's beautiful," Bonnie said, "and I bet she could skate anywhere in the world if she wanted to. I'm going to be just like her."

The first problem came when Mom took us to the hardware store to get Bonnie a larger pair of skates. We left the dog in the station wagon and went into the store to look at their selection. New skates cost so much money. I've had only two new pairs in my life, my first ones when I was two, and a pair when I was four. Bonnie had inherited both these pairs, in fact had just grown out of the four-year size. Because we needed a new pair every one or two years, we usually ended up with second-hand ones.

"We have a pair in your size that were just traded in," the man said. "You're a lucky girl." He rummaged around in the back room and returned with the skates. The blades showed traces of rust as the previous owner hadn't wiped them off properly before putting on the protectors, and the boots were scarred. "Here, try these on."

Tears welled up in Bonnie's eyes. She hid her face in Mom's coat. "I don't like them," she whispered into its folds.

"Stop being such a baby," Mom said sharply. "They'll do just fine. We can't be buying new skates every year. Look at Sherri, she doesn't kick up a fuss over second-hand skates."

"But Sherri's are nicer. They've got shiny blades . . . "

"Sometimes you get lucky. Your next ones may be perfect. I think we should take these for now."

"No!" Bonnie's sobs became louder, causing other customers in the store to turn and stare. The man held the offensive skates in his hand, clearly provoked.

"You have a choice, Bonnie," Mom said. "These skates or nothing."

"I'll wear my old ones."

"You can't. They're too small. They would injure your feet."

"They fit if I don't wear socks in them."

"Your feet would freeze without socks. Now try these on."

Reluctantly Bonnie sat down on a chair and tugged on the skates. I could see she was making every effort to pretend they didn't fit, that something was in the toe, that she couldn't stand properly in them, but Mom and the man knelt to feel how her toes filled the leather boots and both pronounced a perfect fit. Bonnie's eyes were red and puffy and her nose was starting to run. I handed her a Kleenex.

"It's okay," I told her in a low voice as I helped her remove the skates and put on her snowboots. "They'll be fine. When we get them home I'll help you clean them up. We'll put a new coat of white polish on them and take some steel wool to the blades to get the rust off. They'll be nice. Poor little skates . . . never had anybody to look after them before."

She quietened down at that thought and I figured our problems were over until she saw Mom hand the man her old skates, her lovely old skates that had once been mine, that still had shiny silver blades and perfect white boots.

"My skates!" Bonnie cried, and tried to grab them back.

Mom slapped away her hand. "Don't be so greedy, you can't have both. You grow into a new size, you give up the old ones."

Bonnie looked at the two pairs of skates, the shiny old ones the man was already reaching for, and the scuffed pair she must now call her own, and threw back her head and let out a long wail.

"Get this kid out of here," Mom said to me in a harsh whisper. "Take her out to the car while I pay the difference. My goodness, if I had known I'd have *this* to deal with, I'd have sent her with your father. Get her out before we all get thrown out."

I took the scuffed skates, as Bonnie would have nothing to do with them, then grabbed Bonnie's arm and dragged her through the rest of the hardware store, down the sidewalk and into the station wagon. She screamed her head off until Mom came, then threw herself down on the seat and quietly sobbed. The dog lay beside her and consolingly licked away her salty tears.

In a library book I found a picture of Canada's skating star, Karen Magnussen, wearing a five-dollar pair of skates when she was six years old. At age ten Karen won the British Columbia Coast Championship, and went on to win three world gold medals. When she turned professional in 1975, she signed a $300,000 three-year contract with Ice Capades, the largest they had ever offered an ice skater. Bonnie was finally comforted.

We had no problem getting ice time for skating practise in the Gardin and District Indoor Arena. That's the difference between small towns and cities: in the city we would have been practising at outdoor rinks, as ice-time is so expensive there. But in Gardin there were just the hockey teams and the figure skaters to use the ice, and public skaters three nights a week.

Bonnie and I stayed to practise most nights after the others had gone home. Bonnie would set her lips in a straight line, her smile suddenly erased in concentration, as she tried to become an expert in one season.

Together Bonnie and I practised spirals, with me helping her keep her free foot and head at the same level, her back arched, bottom down, hips pressed forward as Miss Wesley had instructed. We skated backward, did split jumps and spread-eagles and sit-spins. Then for fun we did wheelbarrows with Bonnie as the barrow because she was smaller.

Right after Christmas Miss Wesley called us all together to tell us the musical routines she had selected for our carnival. The tiny little kids were doing a number called Winter Wonderland where they were all snowflakes. An older group would be reindeer prancing among the snowflakes. It didn't matter how often the snowflakes fell down or if they forgot their drill formations, for snowflakes can drift anywhere and do anything.

"The six- to eight-year-olds will feature Winter Sports this year," Miss Wesley said. "You will be representing the various things one can do in Gardin during the winter.

"The ten- to twelve-year group is our largest and therefore they will be carrying the show with Ice Flowers. The four senior students will each have a solo . . . "

But I was no longer listening. Ice Flowers. I would be pretty for once. I was tired of being one of Santa's reindeer or a dwarf, like the year we put on Snow White.

I was not prepared for Bonnie's response to the part assigned her in the carnival.

"I won't be a bowling pin!" she cried as I helped her remove her skates. Other kids were looking at her as she wiped her tears away with her wool mitts.

"A bowling pin?" I couldn't help the snicker that escaped. "How can anyone be a bowling pin?"

"I don't know," she wailed. "I don't want to be one! You know what we have to do? The girls are bowling pins and the boys are balls. It's awful! I hate Miss Wesley!" She broke into sobs again as I hurriedly got her into her coat and out into the fresh air.

"Stop bawling," I said as we walked home through the snow. "Your tears will freeze on your face." It was hard to concentrate on her problems while I was imagining myself an ice flower. I would be wearing a sparkling tiara and a shiny satin skating costume.

The night of the carnival was snowy with blizzard warnings, but it didn't seem to affect the crowd. Almost all the seats were filled with parents, brothers, sisters, aunts and uncles, grandparents, neighbours, everyone even remotely connected with the group of eighty or so kids involved in the carnival, or those who just liked a good show.

First there was the Grand March where everyone skated around the rink in a drill formation, the older ones holding Canadian and Albertan flags. We were all dressed in red or blue tights with white tops. It must have looked nice from the seats because the applause was great.

The Winter Wonderland show was next, and we could hear the audience laugh as the little ones forgot where they were to go and skated all over the place, their cumbersome snowflake costumes tipping, parts falling off and littering the ice or trailing behind like tails. The reindeer were obviously annoyed that their intricate jumps and prances brought laughs rather than applause, but the act got the audience into a good mood.

Next came the Winter Sports number, representing hockey, square dancing, sleigh riding and curling. They were all politely applauded. Then came the bowlers. I looked through the curtain as Bonnie and four other girls skated out and bravely positioned themselves as five bowling pins. The music was "Flight of the Bumblebee," a fast-paced tune that seemed to put a speed spirit into the three boys who were the balls. They thundered down the length of the ice, intersecting and doing figure eights around the pins. Down went a pin, spinning on her bottom, as the balls skated on in triumph. Bonnie was the head pin who was to defend her fellow pins from the balls; but when she saw a ball coming toward her, she turned and skated away as fast as she could. The ball followed in hot pursuit. There was an immediate roar of laughter from the audience, followed by cheers for the escaping pin and howls of encouragement for the ball. Finally Bonnie was caught. The ball wobbled in front of her, clearly undecided what he should do. Then she calmly reached out her foot and tripped him. The crowd whistled and jeered, crying "foul!" and "way to go!" The other pins waited, trembling, as the balls skated around them, until the ice was cluttered with pins and balls spinning upon the white cold surface.

The Ice Flowers number was next. We skated out, ten girls and six boys, dressed in brilliant satins. My hair was pinned up in a braided bun, and around my head rested a sparkling rhinestone-encrusted tiara. My satin costume was designed with a tutu of turquoise netting that bounced with my every move. I executed a split jump, remembering to point my toes, and landed perfectly, going into a spread-eagle, both feet on ice, heel to heel, toes pointed in opposite directions. Then we split into pairs doing shadow dances, around and around the ice, the coloured lights flashing on our silver blades and our sparkling tiaras, our costumes shining silkily as they followed our movements, our blades flashing, spinning, never an error, until at last we came to an abrupt halt, frozen in time: Ice Flowers.

The crowd came to their feet, clapping and stamping, their cheers echoing across the vast arena. We stood transfixed in place until the lights came on. We then bowed to our audience and skated regally toward the exit.

I let Bonnie wear my tiara home in the car.

I cannot remember now if she was still perturbed over making her debut on ice as a bowling pin on rusty skates.

This night was mine.

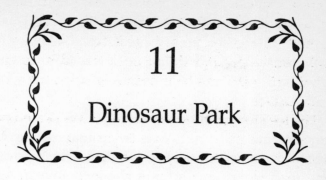

11

Dinosaur Park

"The class is going on a field trip next week," Mr. Johns announced on a bright spring morning in the first week of May. "We're going by school bus to Dinosaur Park."

"Aw, I've seen it a hundred times," Bernard Bazant moaned. "Part of it's on our property."

"You're very fortunate, Bernard. Many here have not had the pleasure of seeing the park. It's still in a natural state but it may not remain that way for long, now being a world historical site. Tourists will be coming, and scientists . . . "

Bernard rolled his eyes. "Here we go again. Open the gates . . . "

"A wonderful array of fossilized remains has been found in the park, although you're not allowed to take anything you find home with you. These fossils must be left for scientists, called paleontologists. Prehistoric reptiles from the Mesozoic era once roamed our land anywhere from 65 to 225 million years ago. We will first study them here in class, then look at the displays in the Interpretive Centre at the site, then explore the valleys and caves ourselves."

We spent the rest of the week studying dinosaurs. They were interesting. We tried to imagine our flat plains once being like a jungle, hot and steamy, lush with leafy trees and ferns and vines, swamps in which all kinds of dinosaurs splashed their gigantic tails.

The day of the trip was bright with spring. We pushed down the bus windows. In rushed cold crisp air, carrying with it the heavy smell of fields emerging from their old winter blanket of snow, of green grass pushing through the brown mat of last year's swath, of spring rivulets surging in the ditches, of roadside bushes greening up with buds.

I sat with Lori and we arranged to go together on this report too, as we had received an A on our last one.

The bus turned off the main highway onto a road that looked no wider than a cow trail. We bumped along for a few miles until the bus came to a sudden halt. I stood up. Cows surrounded the bus, the herd dividing and swarming around us, their brown backs flowing in a steady line below our windows. I wanted to reach out and touch them, but the window was too high. Two cowboys followed the herd, one riding off to the right to keep the cattle from wandering into unfenced fields. They raised their hats as they passed, and yelled a greeting. Both men were Indians with olive-coloured skin and sparkling brown eyes. They wore short, fur-collared jean jackets, with bright scarves around their necks, and leather gloves. We waved and yelled back.

"It's Joe Crazy Cat and Albert Fine Man," Bernard informed us knowingly. "They work for the Bar Twelve. They're just cutting out the herd, getting some steers off to the packers."

"They're Blackfoot Indians," Lori said, "from around Gleichen. We hired them one spring to break some horses."

The bus resumed its travels and we looked out at flat prairies that seemed to stretch to the horizon. Could dinosaurs really have roamed here? I heard a yell and strained to look ahead: in front of us appeared a vista like a biblical city. A canyon stretched perhaps seven miles across. Contained within its bowl were red-brown peaks called hoodoos that jutted high into the sky, then plunged down into deep crevasses. The cliffs were pocked with caves. The morning sun glinted on the hillsides, burning off the dew, causing the layers of sandstone and mudstone to shine like bronze.

The bus slowly made its way down a winding road into the basin of the canyon.

"When we get out, I want you to go straight to the Interpretive Centre," Mr. Johns said. "Nobody is to wander off, do you understand?"

"Yeah, yeah."

We pushed into the aisle, surging ahead, then spilled out of the bus and charged over to the centre. We milled about, looking at pictures and graphs, but we'd studied it all this week. We wanted to explore!

After Mr. Johns dutifully repeated things we already knew, we ran over to see John Ware's cabin. I knew about John Ware from Lori. Her great-grandfather had known him too. John Ware was a black man from South Carolina who had come north on a cattle drive, liked what he saw of Alberta, and decided to stay. He was a big man with a gentle heart, Lori said. He and Sam Howe, another southern Alberta pioneer, had come to the Red Deer River to establish cow ranches; Mr. Ware built his on the south side of the river and lived there for many years. The cozy little cabin where he and his wife had raised their children had been moved onto this site. The big wood stove in the corner looked ready for someone to throw in kindling and start a good fire. Red checkered curtains hung from the windows. I touched the arm of a rocking chair and it gently rocked. The other kids pushed past, eager to get outside and let off some energy.

I stayed behind, wandering into the sitting room to read details of the Wares' lives from plaques on the wall.

"You'd have liked him real good. My grandfather always said he was a good neighbour." I turned to see Bernard Bazant standing beside me. "He was here when my grandfather started his ranch,"

Bernard said. "Grandpa used to tell us how hard it was to live in this country in the early days. One winter there was a blizzard that didn't let up for six days. They couldn't go out to check the cattle or nothing, couldn't go past the door. When the blizzard finally let up, my grandfather got out by crawling through a window, then shovelled the snow away so they could get the door open. Most of the cattle died. They were all piled into one corner of the barbed-wire fence, standing on their feet, dead."

Bernard's face was solemn and serious. I was about to speak to him, to tell him how awful that must have been, when his face changed and he became the Bernard I knew from class:

"Yeah, they were all goners," he said, "udders froze right off the cows, standing there. Tits froze right into the snow." He turned and was gone.

I stomped outside, annoyed that I'd given him a moment's doubt, and told Lori what Bernard had said about the cows.

"That's right, Sherri," Lori said. "It's an awful thing to see. We lost a bunch of animals one winter too. It's pretty grotesque . . . some horses had their tails and manes chewed off from starvation. Others had no hair left on their legs . . . "

"Okay, I believe you . . . and Bernard. I guess I'm just a city kid. We never see anything like that."

"Lucky you," she said.

The class was waiting for everyone to catch up so we could go exploring. Mr. Johns was well into his spiel about watching for rattlesnakes. Although none would be out this early in the year, he felt it his duty to warn us. Also about climbing too high on the cliffs and about seventeen other dangers he thought up. I guess teachers have a lot of responsibility when they take kids on field trips. And this place looked ripe for accidents.

The spring sun became warmer as the morning wore on. Soon we had our jackets tied around our waists. Some kids asked if they could go barefoot, to which Mr. Johns gave a resounding "No!" Lori and I lagged behind, being more interested than most of the kids who charged along the path in a hurry to get nowhere.

Lori had brought her camera, so we took pictures of a hawk sweeping over the valley, its wings still, its body streamlined and swift. We took turns standing against the cliff walls as she took my picture, then I took hers. We asked Mr. Johns to take one of us together, which we would keep forever to show how long we'd been best friends.

"Let's ask if we can explore that cave," Lori said, pointing to a dark hole high on the hill above where we stood.

"Only if you're careful and don't take chances," Mr. Johns said. "I think it's actually a tunnel. It comes out on the far side of the hill."

We clambered up the dry clay hillside, holding onto tufts of prairie wool and small shrubs, careful not to grab onto a hidden cactus. We reached the cave entrance and turned around for a full view of the hoodoos and gullies, crags and cliffs that surrounded us. They peaked and dropped, following the blue cut of the Red Deer River.

The cave was dimly lit, curving in a semi-circle to its exit on the other side of the hill. We examined the walls for signs of fossils and found some of leaves and small shells like snails. It was cool and quiet in the cave. We sat down to absorb the feel of its ancient secrets, leaning our backs against the curved wall.

"Do you think dinosaurs were cold-blooded or warm-blooded?" Lori asked.

"I don't know. Some of our books call them reptiles, others call them mammals. They hatched from eggs, so they couldn't really be mammals. It must have been neat to live here then."

"Humans didn't live at the same time dinosaurs existed. Those movies and stuff that show cavemen slaying dinosaurs aren't real. Humans didn't show up until the Cenozoic era."

Suddenly we heard a noise, a deep growl, barely discernible over our conversation. I felt the sound more than I heard it; a strange sensation travelled through my back pressed against the cave wall. I sat up straight and looked over at Lori. Her eyes were round and staring toward the gloom of the back of the cave.

"Did you hear that?" I whispered.

"I . . . think so."

Again we heard the slightest sound, like a moan, followed by a scratching noise. We slowly rose to our feet, crouching against the wall. My hands felt moist against the cool wall; I could feel my heart racing, beating against my shirt. Lori started backing toward the cave entrance. Suddenly I felt a rush of air and two bodies came charging from the dark end of the cave, two large black objects that beat their wings and cried in high-pitched wails. We were frozen to the spot.

Bernard Bazant and Jim Morrow flung themselves at us, trying to wrestle us to the ground. With jackets held over their heads and their arms thrust out, they appeared like pterodactyls, extinct flying reptiles with wings like bats.

"You stupid idiots, you scared us to death!" Lori flew at Jim, her arms beating at his out-flung bat wings. "How could you be so rotten?"

My heart was beating so hard I could barely catch my breath. Bernard stood in the shadows, his head down, his cheekbones highlighted by the shaft of light coming in from the cave's entrance.

"Hey, I'm sorry," he mumbled. "We didn't think you'd freak out. We were just fooling around."

"Do you know how creepy this place makes me feel?" My voice croaked like a toad's. "Sitting here among fossils millions of years old, talking about reptiles and . . . oh, you just make me so mad! Get out of here."

Bernard took my arm, more gently than he had a moment ago during his pterodactyl act, and tried to guide me toward the far end of the cave. "Come back here, I want you to see something."

"No."

"Honest, Sherri, I won't hurt you. I found something you will be interested in. Come on."

I looked back at Lori, who was still giving Jim a piece of her mind. They had gone outside the cave and were standing on the rough grass that covered the hillside. They didn't seem to be worried about me.

"I don't know," I said doubtfully, but Bernard tugged my arm, then went ahead to where the cave rounded toward its final exit. I followed.

He reached nearly to the back exit of the cave, then bent down and picked up a small object. "Here," he said, handing it to me like a present. I took it in my hand. It was heavy like a stone, but it had a peculiar formation. I scraped away some soft sand, and two jagged prongs emerged.

"I think it's a tooth," he said. "Maybe a dinosaur's tooth. You can have it."

I sat down at the side of the cave and examined it. Yes, it was a tooth, very very old and hardened like rock, about the size of a golf ball. I polished it against my jacket. Bernard Bazant smiled at me, and his slate-grey eyes held a warmth and softness I had never noticed before.

"I can't keep it," I said. "Mr. Johns said we weren't to take anything from here. It's against the law."

"Well . . . I found it and I'm giving it to you."

I looked at Bernard and smiled. "I'll tell you what. Let's bury it here. There are probably other teeth and bones buried here, and someday they'll be discovered by the scientists. Okay?"

"Like a secret?"

"Yeah . . . sure."

"Like *our* secret." Bernard was kneeling beside me. His presence seemed to fill the cave, making me nervous and edgy.

"I guess so."

We sat in silence as I buried the tooth in the soft sandstone of the cave floor. The only sounds that could be heard were Bernard's even breathing and the occasional cry of a bird from outside the cave.

"We'd better be getting back," I said. "Mr. Johns will be wondering where we are."

Bernard rose, offering me his hand. I didn't know what else to do so I took it, and he helped me to my feet. We walked out of the cave into the dazzle of bright-blue sky, to the voices of thirty kids yelling that it was time for lunch.

We boarded the school bus after lunch, and I found Bernard pushing into the seat beside me. I looked around. No one had noticed. I saw that some other kids had paired up. What was going on? Sure, it was broad daylight, but wouldn't Mr. Johns say something?

I sat back and looked out the window as the bus loaded with kids, now quiet, their energy spent racing up the hills and down the gullies of Dinosaur Park. I didn't want to talk. I wanted to think about this strange place, to keep it in my memory, keep the colours of copper cliffs and blue spring sky forever alive, so I could recreate them like an artist mixing colours on a palette. I wanted to retain the smells of new grass and early crocuses, sage and dry caves, the sight of brown cattle streaming past our bus, the sound of the Indian herdsmen ki-yipping past on galloping horses. I wanted to remember the sound of Bernard's low voice as we talked in the cave, the strange sensation I felt when he knelt beside me, the firmness of his hand as he helped me to my feet.

Because even then I had the feeling I might never experience these things again, that we wouldn't be here for much longer, that my days in the wild west were quickly coming to a close.

12

Resolution

The men from next door moved out the middle of May.

Bonnie and I stood on my bed, watching out the back window as they loaded their mattresses and old chairs onto the pickup, which they had backed up to the steps. Scarface had got the Ford Bronco running and had taken it away, leaving behind the burrowed indentations made by the dogs during their winter imprisonment. One of the men noticed us looking out the window. He neither smiled nor frowned.

A minute later we heard a knock on the door.

"We're taking off," I heard the man say to Mom. "Could we leave a couple of things with you? Someone'll be back for them in a week or so."

"I guess that would be all right," Mom said, and we heard the man's feet clump down the stairs, carrying in his excess belongings.

I jumped off the bed and went to the top of the

stairs, hanging over the wrought-iron railing to await his emergence from our basement. "Where are the dogs?" I asked as soon as he appeared.

He looked up, startled. "Dogs? Oh, they were Pete's. He's gone up to Faro in the Yukon. I don't know who's got them now." And with that, he was gone.

I hadn't realized until now that Scarface had a name. Pete. We would never see him again, or the dogs. They had all disappeared, like names erased from a blackboard.

"Come on!" Bonnie rushed past me down the basement to see what the men had left. We stared at the boxes piled in one corner next to the hot-water tank: a cardboard box of plastic unmatched dishes, a set of cheap pots and pans black with misuse, and a box of duck decoys.

At the end of May Dad came home and said he had been offered a job with a meat packing plant in Calgary. Now we were moving in circles. Perhaps we had a pattern after all.

"We'll stay until school is finished," Mom announced. "I want the girls to complete at least one year in the same place." She looked at us, willing our support. "You can both help pack. It won't take long."

Dad found a house to rent in Calgary and moved into it, taking just enough furniture to get by. He phoned nearly every night, telling us how happy he was with his job, about his chances to get ahead, how we would like the area he had chosen for us to live. It was near a playground, he said, and only two blocks from the elementary and junior high schools.

I'll be in junior high next year, I thought with amazement. I'll practically be grown up. A teenager. I looked at Bonnie, pitying her for the years that stretched ahead.

Lori had told me animals and people experience similar social situations. I remembered the time we were sitting on a corral fence with Buck, after Bill, Bob and Buck had unsaddled their horses and turned them into the corral. We watched the horses mill around inside the corral, uneasy until a lord and master was agreed upon. The rest then found their places accordingly, at varying distances from the water and oat troughs.

"Chickens are the same. They'll peck each other until the leader gets the best roosts," Lori said. Her simple explanation took away the evil somehow, making the human problem of fitting in sound natural. I had turned to Buck, who was sitting silently on the top pole of the corral fence, rolling a smoke. "Is it really the same with people?" I asked.

"Sure is," Buck said slowly, his hazel eyes looking wise and a little sad. "You've got to roll with the punches in this old world."

We watched Bill and Bob's bow-legged stride as they ambled toward the bunkhouse, slapping their thighs with their old hats, causing dust to puff. The two old cowboys looked tired and a little stooped. I guess everyone has his share of tough times.

June came in hot and dry, like mid-summer. One day I was in the basement getting some packing boxes when I heard a squeaking noise at the window. I dragged a box over and looked outside. Three baby gophers were peering from their hole a few inches from the basement window, their bright little eyes taking in the big world for the first time.

I stepped quietly from the box and called upstairs to Bonnie. "Quiet, now, just stand here and look out."

She stared at the gophers in silent wonderment. "Won't you miss this, Sherri?" she asked in a voice just above a whisper. "When we move to the city, I mean. I bet there's no gophers in Calgary."

"Sure there will be," I assured her. "We'll just have to go looking for them."

June 28 was circled on our calendar, a big yellow ring around the date, like sun dogs. On the last day of school I got everyone to sign our class picture, some putting their addresses on the back so I could write to them. Mr. Johns wished me well and said I had potential as a writer because I expressed detail so well in my reports.

"I'll miss you, Sherri," Lori said as we sat on the school steps under the shade of the black poplar trees.

"Maybe you can come in some weekend, stay with us in Calgary."

"Maybe."

I didn't expect she would, though. Her family didn't often go to the city. There was nothing they needed there. Already she had been practising every night after school for gymkhana and junior rodeo competitions, and her summer was lined up with rodeos and community picnics and other events I would have had no part in even if we had been staying.

"Here." She handed me a flat parcel wrapped in coloured tissue paper.

"What's this?"

"A present. For you leaving." She looked away, embarrassed, and I thought she wasn't so different from Bill, Bob and Buck. Their kindness and their feelings went so deep, while on the surface their expressions never seemed to change.

I unwrapped the parcel and held the present on my knees. A book of pictures of the Old West by Charles M. Russell, who had been a friend of Lori's great-grandfather in the early 1900s. They had worked together in Havre, Montana, then met again at the first Calgary Stampede in 1912, Lori said. The Swensons referred to him as Charlie. That's why Lori got such good marks in social studies: her family was part of our history.

I flipped the pages to see a hunting party of Indians riding pellmell over the prairies, their arrows poised to bring down the stumbling buffalo, cowboys dust-covered from hundred-mile trail

rides, horses snorting and wheeling as they cut
herds. I could smell the prairie, feel its heat and
dust, its freshness after a rain, its numbing mid-
winter cold, hear its howling winds that sang of
times gone by.

"Don't forget us," Lori said quickly, then ran to
catch her bus.

I was still sitting on the steps, holding the book,
when I felt a nudge on my shoulder. I looked up to
see Bernard Bazant standing beside me.

"So you're leavin'." He looked out over the school
yard as if interested in something on the far side of
the lawn.

"Yeah. Tomorrow."

"You're crazy. Who'd want to live in the city? It's
boring."

"To some, maybe. I'm from there."

"Yeah?"

"Yeah. My family . . . was part of its history."

"Oh. Well, see you sometime, eh? Don't fall down
a manhole."

And he was gone to catch his bus out to his
family's ranch, to work like a man all summer, to
come back to school in the fall inches taller, huskier,
bronzed from the sun. I willed my mind to stop
thinking about it.

The moving truck came early in the morning, and
by the time it left it was lunch time. Mom took us
down to the Kentucky Fried Chicken, the first time

we'd been there since the night we moved to Gardin almost a year ago.

We returned to the empty echoing house to do a final cleaning, vacuuming dust from corners, wiping windowsills stained grey with swirls of prairie dust. Then we loaded the bucket and mop, vacuum and plants into the station wagon. The dog jumped into the back and peered at us through the philodendron. Construction equipment roared through the neighbourhood as crews arrived to finally pave the rutted street.

"Good-bye, house," Bonnie sang. "Good-bye, yard, good-bye, doggies."

I looked straight ahead as we drove past the school yard, through the downtown area, so small and compact, past Jamie's trailer court. A month after he'd moved I had received a postcard from him, showing a picture of a polar bear. It was postmarked "Churchill, Manitoba," but he gave no address, so I couldn't write him back. I closed my eyes, blocking out the passing stores and gas stations.

"Good-bye, Lori and Duchess and Flame, good-bye, Bill, Bob and Buck, good-bye, Bernard Bazant, you big ugly gorilla," I said silently.

The prairie on the edge of town stretched green and inviting, sending us smells of summer grasses and flowers. Through the open window I could hear the songs of meadowlarks and the ticking of grasshoppers.

Mom stopped as we reached the Trans-Canada

highway, then turned west toward Calgary. Soon we would be with Dad again, hearing about his wonderful new job, seeing our new school. But that wouldn't start for two whole months.

We picked up speed as we passed the packing plant and the feed-lot on the opposite side, the dreadful smell of silage warning us of its existence. Then we were into the country, the range lands of southern Alberta. Green hills rolled forever beneath a cloudless blue sky. Heat waves shimmered in zig-zags from the pavement.

We turned north onto highway 36 toward Hanna, a more scenic and less crowded route than the Trans-Canada. Wild roses lined the ditches, sending out their delicate sun-warmed fragrance.

The station wagon rolled silently down a long curving hill, down a gully cleft by the smooth brown waters of the Red Deer River. We were not far from the Swenson place.

I noticed first a bright pile of clothes, then saw horses tethered on the bank. I could hear shouts. Mom slowed the car and peered toward the sound.

Three naked cowboys splashed about in the brown sparkling water of the river, two older men and one young man. They were throwing clumps of mud at one another, laughing, diving, their bodies sleek as seals. The young man clambered up onto the muddy bank, water flying from his dark hair in crystal sprays. I saw his brown face and arms, tanned from the hot sun, his fish-white body and legs, then he was gone from my view as the station wagon rounded a wide curve in the highway.

I was given but one second of time to see his face. I wondered if he still had a broken heart.

I leaned back against the vinyl cushions of the car and succumbed to a wave of sadness.

The book of Charlie Russell's paintings lay open on my lap. I traced my fingers over the taut muscles of his sweating horses. The smell of wild roses drifted in, overpowering and sweet. In the distance I thought I could still hear the cowboys' yells.

I closed my eyes, calling up my own images: prong-horned antelope dancing over the prairie, a camouflaged coyote trotting down a path in the gully, the squeak of gophers, the tick of grasshoppers, the empty howl of a husky on a cold winter night, the powerful surge of a horse called Flame propelling me over the rolling plains. Lean ki-yipping Indians astride galloping horses, herding hundreds of bawling cattle. Cowboys with broken hearts.

I could keep them alive forever, if I could paint pictures.

About the Author

Shirlee Smith Matheson was born in Winnipeg, Manitoba. She is married, with two daughters.

Having lived in about twenty places, she well understands the adjustments encountered in moving: making new friends in new schools and leaving familiar things behind. Her rural experiences provide much of the material for her writing.

Shirlee is an alumna of the Banff Centre's writing program, and winner of a number of awards. Her articles and short stories have appeared in magazines across Canada and in the United States. She writes and publishes non-fiction and fiction books, as well as stage plays, for adult and juvenile markets. She presently resides with her family in Calgary.